The riders were spilling into the street, and they came as Texas men had always come, at a high lope and with the guns banging . . .

They came as the trail drovers of another day had come to Sedalia and Abilene and Dodge City and all the trail towns, crowding their horses and loosing their thunder; and the false fronts of Tamerlane caught the sounds and sent them beating back in growing waves, and horsemen were everywhere, and their rallying cry went up, "Hammer! Hammer!" It was the name of Carradine's ranch.

They spread out, encompassing the night street, and the thunder of guns rolled over Tamerlane . . .

Colonel Carradine was at the center of the chaos Hammer wrought. He sat a rearing, pitching saddle almost directly below the drugstore; light fell upon him, and his white hair was flying, and his goatee bristled a great defiance. He was power and invincibility, and the people of Tamerlane quailed before him.

He had come to break Brian Ives out of jail. For one of his own—even Brian Ives—he would hold the street, daring anyone to stop him, to raise a gun at him and aim . . .

12-09

Books by Norman A. Fox

Shadow on the Range
The Thirsty Land

Published by POCKET BOOKS

NORMAN A. FOX

Shadow On The Range

POCKET BOOKS
New York London Toronto Sydney Tokyo

This book is a work of fiction. Names, characters, places and incidents are either the product of the author's imagination or are used fictitiously. Any resemblance to actual events or locales or persons, living or dead, is entirely coincidental.

POCKET BOOKS, a division of Simon & Schuster Inc.
1230 Avenue of the Americas, New York, N.Y. 10020

Published by arrangement with Dodd, Mead & Co.

ISBN: 0-671-64817-9

First Pocket Books printing July 1988

10 9 8 7 6 5 4 3 2 1

POCKET and colophon are trademarks of Simon & Schuster Inc.

Printed in the U.S.A.

For a Friend o' Mine,
Wayne D. Overholser

1

Tamerlane

THE TOWN WAS CALLED TAMERLANE AND THIS WAS ITS only individuality, for it was all the towns of all the prairies, a flat and dusty clutter of buildings, vainglorious with false-fronting. Horses had known Tamerlane; they had stirred the dust of its single street and gnawed the hitch-rails and left their droppings to gather flies. Cattle had known Tamerlane, too; they had spilled northward from the grazed-out Texas plains and butted at the wooden porch supports of a raw new town as they had been hazed through to Montana's thousand hills. And men—uncurried men, given to thick bullhide chaps and the promiscuous use of Colonel Colt's invention. They were here yet, the horses and the cattle and the men; but their sun was setting.

A man who had known all three before he had turned his hands to other things could find a sadness in the sight of Tamerlane after the years, and it was thus with young Dr. Brian Ives. A railroad had fetched him to the end of an aimless spur, a stagecoach had covered the last miles, and he stood before the stage depot in the afternoon's heat, seeing horse-and-rope men who jingled their spurs along the planking, but seeing, too, the calico and the denim of people who broke the sod. Some inward thought brought a bleakness to his eyes, but his sigh was an acceptance of the change, and in this moment he was wise and kindly and tolerant.

At his feet sat his carpetbag and his instrument case; he had brought no more than these, and they held the last decade of his life locked in them. He had not been one to lay his hands on wordly goods, and even the Prince Albert coat, accepted garb of the professional man of his day, was worn thin at the elbows. The coat gave him an added tallness—he topped six feet and was inclined to stoop—but it was his face that people remembered. He wasn't handsome, but people could put their trust in him, and sometimes those who thought they had known him before remembered photographs of the young Abraham Lincoln in his Springfield years and realized where the resemblance lay. His eyes were gray and grave, his hair brown and unruly; and the razor was a habit with him.

The coach that had brought him had wheeled on around to the wagon yard, and there was no one here to meet Ives. He'd expected that. He picked the two bags from the planking and headed toward the livery stable—he could rent a buggy—but he took his time, letting the town soak into him, letting the old, remembered things make their impact. He walked unrecognized; he had expected that, too. But when he saw a man seated on the edge of the boardwalk, his feet a tangle before him, he said, "Hello, Charley," making an experiment of it.

Here was the town drunk, a gnarled and useless man, but one who had time for remembering, and Charley lifted his red-streaked eyes and looked long and hard and said, "Ives—Brian Ives," as though not believing it. But Ives had paced onward. Abreast of the Oriental Café, he looked back and saw that Charley was lurching diagonally across the dust of the street; Charley had found something to make this day different from the days before it; Charley had news.

Ives smiled; and because he was a man whose thoughts always turned inward, he told himself that he'd been childish.

He got to the livery, and there was no one in its shadowy depth; the horses stood listlessly in their stalls; the air was heavy with the smell of them, and this was somehow reassuring, this finding the stable unchanged. He lingered here, a man in a quiet, timeless eddy; beyond was the street and the steady current of reality, and he stepped back into it reluctantly. A wagon rolled along, a man and a woman upon its seat, a horde of children in the box behind, seated gingerly amidst the cargo. Spooled barbed wire glinted in the sun.

Across the street came three men, all of them long-striding, but at once only one counted, and he was in the lead. He was young and clean-shaven and golden blond; and Ives had never seen him before. He wore wool pants and a belted six-shooter, and his hat was a cowboy's, though not so broad-brimmed as most; yet he was not of the ranch breed. How Ives knew this, he couldn't have said; perhaps it was the walk of the youngster. He looked like a man with business on his mind, and his eyes were on Ives, but he had not called out, so Ives put his back to him and headed along the street. He was abreast of the Congress Saloon and across the street from the drugstore when the youngster said, "Hold up a minute, Ives!"

Ives stopped and turned around and said, "Yes?"

"You came in on the stage awhile ago?" the youngster said.

He, too, had stopped, taking a slaunch-wise stand and hooking his thumbs in the gun belt; and the stance was so affected that it made Ives smile. Yet there was a danger in this youngster; it lay deep in his eyes; they were coldly blue and too old for his years. His companions were older men, both of them in bib overalls, and one had a ragged beard. They might have been wearing tags proclaiming them farmers. Ives knew again that only the youngster counted, and Ives set down his bags, wanting his hands free, and remembered then that the only gun he'd ever owned was locked inside the carpetbag.

He said, "Yes, I came in on the stage."

"It leaves again this evening," the youngster said. "Be on it."

Ives made his voice placid. "Couldn't I stay until tomorrow?"

The youngster's face softened—Ives had wanted to see if it would—and then the steel was in the boy's eyes again. "Tonight," he said firmly. "Be sure about that."

Ives thought: *Here it is, already,* and wished for his gun again; and then he saw the fourth man. He was across the street, lounging in the shade of a doorway a few buildings up from the drugstore, a square-cut man with a brutish hunch to his shoulders. This sort of maneuvering was older than grass, and Ives had known the pattern before he'd known the Latin that went into a prescription; and a silent laughter was in him, and the headiness of crowding danger. And perverseness, too. He placed the flat of his palms against the chest of the youngster and shoved him hard into the arms of the two behind, and at the same time Ives went down to one knee, expecting the man across the street to start the shooting.

The youngster rebounded from the two who'd caught him, a heady anger tearing all thinking out of him, and a man in a window above the drugstore said then, "Break it up, Cory!"

His was a voice out of nowhere, the unexpected, the sixth ace in a stacked game; and the youngster, Cory, stopped in his wild lunge and looked up; and so did Ives. The window framed a face that might have been a rising moon, round and fat and jovial, the eyes lost in folds of flesh, the lips wide and rubbery and grinning; but it was the shotgun that Ives saw first. The man behind it said again, "Break it up, Cory! This old Parker is loaded with wagon bolts and broken bottles, and they'd have to bury you in a basket." And then, with equal affability, "Howdy, Doc. Welcome home."

Ives said, "Hello, Stoll. You're certainly in the right place at the right time!"

Cory picked his hat from where it had fallen, and his gaze held the piled-up hatred of these past few moments. He looked at Ives and said, "I've been pushed before. I've always found the time and place to push back. That goes for you, and it goes for Colonel Carradine, when you see him."

Ives said, "I'll tell him that."

Cory turned on his heel and strode away, the two wordlessly following after him. Ives looked for the square-cut man in the doorway; he had vanished. From the window, Stoll said, "Come on up and pass the time of day, Doc. You remember the layout? The stairs are at the back of the drugstore."

Ives said, "I'll find them."

He came across the street and entered the drugstore; here was something out of his own way of life, and in the cool darkness of the place he again found the old and remembered, and something else as well, something that erased what had happened just now, something that said: *You are Brian Ives, physician and surgeon, a man who knows only the violence wrought by others, having no personal part in it yourself.* Yet his palms still tingled from the shoving of Cory, and he could remember the twin barrels of the shotgun commanding the street.

A clerk, pimpled and adolescent, was behind the counter, and to him Ives nodded, skirting the shelves and knowing what they held without looking. Prussian Worm Powder for horses. Salt-Vet, the cow remedy. Dr. Shoop's Rheumatic Remedy. Thus could the needs of the three be attended to; and there were the bottled medicines and the vari-colored glass jars with the ingredients that made up into prescriptions. Ives swung past these and ascended the stairs, and Marco Stoll met him with a plump hand extended and said again, "Howdy, Doc. Welcome home."

The living-quarters of the man were overfurnished and repulsive with mohair, a marble-topped table centering the room with a chessboard laid out; but it was the man, Marco Stoll, who filled the cramped space. He wasn't tall, no more than five feet seven, but his girth was enormous, and he crowded his clothes and waddled when he walked. He waved Ives to a chair and took one for himself and said, "Whatever fetched you back here, Doc? It's been ten years, hasn't it?"

"Ten," Ives said. "One year knocking about. One year reading medicine under a preceptor who took a fancy to me in Wyoming. Reading medicine! Most of my time was spent with a broom. Two years in medical school. The last few I've been practicing in Oregon."

"Like that country?"

Ives shrugged. "It's something like Montana. Only the sagebrush grows higher. And there are lava caves. And the mountains and the prairies seem to blend into one." He looked through the open window; he could see across a rooftop; he could see the shadowy lift of the Sombra Hills, and not until then was he glad to be back.

Stoll burrowed deeper into his chair. He wore black trousers and a black vest and a white shirt with black sleeve-protectors, and he was a toad of a man. "You've built up a nice practice?"

"It takes in a lot of country," Ives said. "I'm a saddlebag sawbones who spends more time riding than counting pulses. And sometimes I take my pay in potatoes."

He felt Stoll's eyes on the shabby Prince Albert, and his thought was that he wasn't fooling this man; Stoll could read what there was to read, and Ives said defensively, *"I* like it. A city practice would stifle a range-reared man."

"Yes," Stoll said, "you had elbowroom on the Hammer, and that would have become habit with you. You didn't say why you came back."

There was Stoll's question again; and into Ives came a faint animosity at this persistence, and the first speculation as to whether more than curiosity prompted it. He looked at Stoll with a man's eyes; Ives had been a fifteen-year-old when last he'd seen Stoll, and he saw that there was a greater depth to Stoll than he'd previously perceived. The man had the twang of cattledom to his speech, yet he was using another language now, and Ives guessed that Stoll had still a third for the talking a man does within himself. He recalled vaguely that Stoll had long ago been a cowboy; he had come up from Texas with the great influx, and that seemed incongruous when you tried picturing Stoll on a horse. Stoll's question still hung in the air, and Ives was remembering that Stoll had likely saved his life.

"Tana sent for me," he said.

Stoll raised his eyebrows; they were dust-colored, giving him a naked look. "So?" he said and was reflective for a moment. "She comes in sometimes. It's through her that I kept track of you." He smiled. "And now it's *Doctor* Ives."

"I had a little trouble getting used to it myself," Ives said.

"Tana told you of the trouble?"

Again that faint animosity touched Ives's nerves, but he said, "The colonel is getting old. And cantankerous. Tana thought I could be of help to him. Yes, she hinted of trouble." He gestured toward the street. "Apparently she knew what she was talking about. Who was that young fire-eater?"

"Cory Lund," Stoll said. "There are a lot of nesters along the upper Sombra. An oldster who looks as though he stepped right out of the Old Testament is the leader of them. Elisha Lund. He believes that a soft answer turneth away wrath. Young Cory, his cub, hasn't lived long enough to learn that."

"He had me rigged good and tight," Ives said. "Across the street was a square-cut fellow with a pair of shoulders that would do credit to an ox."

Stoll frowned. "That would be Brule. He's a saddle-bum who drifted in. I can't believe he'd be sitting in on Cory's game."

"Old Charley recognized me earlier," Ives mused. "He went legging it to spread the word. I suppose that's what set this Cory prowling for me. But how do I count in his scheme of things?"

"Colonel Carradine is crowding the nesters, Doc. It's the old, old story of big rancher and small rancher, except that the colonel can't see that his fight is lost before it starts. Washington has grown tired of the antics of big operators who think they're lords of the earth because they happened to be here first. The day of the open range is over. The law favors the covered wagon over the chuck wagon any day. But Carradine's talking of importing gunmen and making a wholesale cleanup. It could be Johnson County all over again. Carradine should have learned a lesson from Wyoming."

Ives said slowly, "So that's what Tana was worrying about."

Stoll said, "You don't owe a thing to Colonel Carradine. Yes, he raised you, and he educated you after a fashion. But it was bitter bread he gave you to eat. And you just about worked your way through medical school. All the help you ever got from him you paid for in sweat before you left Hammer."

Ives said sharply, "You seem to know a great deal about it."

Stoll gestured toward the window. "In my hours off, I sit there. I see what goes on in Tamerlane. Quite a name for a cowtown, isn't it? There's my balcony seat to this section of the world. The rest of the time I'm behind a counter. People talk. I listen. And I always had my eye on you, Doc. Maybe I felt sorry for you when you were a youngster. Maybe you were worth watching. I'm proud of you."

Ives let the rancor run out of him, and he said, "I'm glad you were at that window today, Stoll."

Stoll spread his fat hands. "I play no sides. This will be a sodbuster town in the long run. As it grows, I'll grow with it. When Cory Lund has cooled off, he'll see that I did *him* a favor, too." He smiled. "Are you going to set up practice here, Doc?"

Ives said, "I'm going to Hammer and find out what it is Tana thinks I can do. Then I'm going to do it. You were right about the bitter bread, Stoll; but Colonel Carradine was as much of a father as I ever had. I've learned a few things since I took to doctoring. One of them is that all the ills aren't of the flesh."

Stoll shook his head. "You pulled yourself up out of here by the roots. You've made a new life for yourself, and you've told me that you like it. Cory Lund's advice wasn't bad, even though it was given in belligerency. He hates Colonel Carradine and I suppose he's heard that you're a sort of foster son of Carradine's. Let me give you the same advice. Take that stage out tonight. You can't live the colonel's life for him."

Ives shook his head. "This is something I can't turn my back on. I'm heading for Hammer as soon as I can rent a buggy. Tana didn't come to meet me. I don't think she wanted the colonel to know she's sent for me."

Stoll sighed. "If you must go, you're welcome to my buggy. I keep it in the livery-stable yard. You can have one of the Hammer hands fetch it back. Carradine has never allowed me to set foot on Hammer, but he shouldn't object to my horse."

Ives said, "Thanks," and came to his feet.

Stoll crossed to the chessboard. "If you must stay, it will be nice having you here. There's been no doctor since old Doc Ellenberg died." He glanced at the board. "Do you favor this game?"

Ives grinned. "I understand it's for brainy people."

Stoll sighed again. "I've played alone for a long time."

"I'll send the buggy back soon," Ives said and walked toward the door. Stoll still stood by the table, his fingers caressing one of the chessmen. It was a pawn; Stoll raised his hand to wave a farewell to Ives, and his fingernail flicked the pawn and it fell, spilling half a dozen others.

2

The Road to Hammer

STOLL'S BUGGY WAS THE SQUARE BOX TYPE, DIRECT OFF-spring of the storied one-horse shay, and Ives had owned one like it in Oregon, using it where there were roads and when the snow wasn't piled too high. His carpetbag and instrument case stowed beneath the seat, he tooled the buggy out of the wagon yard and along the street, Marco Stoll giving him a lift of his hand from the window as Ives passed below. At the town's edge, penned cattle bawled ceaselessly; a dog gave barking, furious escort to Ives this far and no farther; the town fell behind, and Ives took the road north to Hammer and was alone with the prairie and the clatter of wheels and the drum of the horse's hoofs.

The land wore a stark tawniness and seemed flat as a plate and endless beneath the vaulting sky, but that was a deception born of great distance; there were low hills to hump over and coulees to skirt, and yonder, to the west, a palisade of willows, following the windings of Sombra River, shut off the horizon. Yet there was space enough to put a mood in Ives for hurrying, and he used the whip until this urge wore off and an old patience had its way with him again. He drove with no conscious thought, studying the habits of Stoll's horse against any future need for such knowledge; he drove with a bleak aloneness.

And then, suddenly, he was afraid.

A man should be able to put a name to his fear, but there was no name for this one, yet it came from the country, he supposed. There was no other accounting for it. They told tales of Easterners who came visiting and found themselves suddenly possessed of a primitive terror at all the bigness, all the emptiness of Montana; but that couldn't hold true for him. He'd been born to this land. He'd known country like it all of his days, except for the medical school years. Oregon had been something like this; he'd told Marco Stoll so, less than an hour ago. And he'd seen similar country from train and stagecoach, and it hadn't touched him, not this way.

He turned this over in his mind, making his own diagnosis, for here was a cardinal rule to be applied: you found the source before you effected the cure. Then he remembered the penned cattle and their piteous bawling.

Deep in every man lies his first conscious memory, and this was his—cattle bawling beneath a darkling sky. He had never heard a milk cow lowing in the dusk since without multiplying the sound a thousand times and harking up that old memory. But if that was the first link in some ancient chain, the others were missing; there was nothing to tie this to, yet the fear was born from it. It had risen up to haunt him before; he shook it out of his mind now and was angry with himself.

A man should be able to dredge up something better than fear from his homecoming. He'd ridden these prairies as a small boy, he'd got his first schooling in Tamerlane, his formative years had belonged to this land. They should hold a wealth of memory. Yet there was nothing from those years worth the cherishing; he'd buried them under a layer of other years, and until Tana's letter had come he'd been satisfied to leave them buried. Two men had told him to take the stage out tonight. It would be an easy thing to do, and he was of a mind to do it. Yet he kept the buggy headed north, crossing the familiar land, and the old years burst through again like land tossed up by an earthquake.

The school in Tamerlane and the teacher—what had been her name?—and that ancient, crazy jingle, "As I was going to St. Ives, I met a man with seven wives—" Her starchy voice. "Do you know where St. Ives is, children?" Blank, bored looks; eyes with a longing for the out of doors. "Brian, your name is Ives. Probably once, long ago, the name was St. Ives, but the first part of it was dropped. What sort of name is Ives, Brian?"

A self-conscious flaming through him from suddenly being the focus of attention. His childish voice quavering in his ears. "I—I don't know."

"You don't know anything about your own name?" A patronizing smile. "Come now, Brian!"

And then, later, a boy daring the invincibility of that gray ghost of a man, Colonel Carradine. "I'd like to know, sir, who my people were."

The gray ghost coming to a sudden stiffness, a white scar on a man's forehead flaming red. "Don't ever ask me that! Don't ever ask me that again!"

And here were the old years laid bare today.

He used the buggy whip again, lifting the horse to a run, and he kept at this pace until he saw the straying saddler. A range horse is trained to stand when the reins are dropped to the ground, but this horse—a buckskin gelding—was dragging its reins and grazing along; and Ives stopped the buggy and considered this phenomenon. The road had swung nearer the Sombra; over where the willows fringed the stream, there was a gay splashing; and

Ives smiled, understanding. Some cowboy was easing the heat of the day by having himself a swim, and his horse had strayed meanwhile. Thinking this, Ives pulled the buggy to the side of the road and dropped the iron weight with its leather strap and climbed from the vehicle.

He approached the horse gingerly, afraid it would bolt, but the animal let him come to its head and get a hand on the bridle. He saw then that the saddle was old and dilapidated and the horse itself too heavy-bodied to be much of a specimen. There was no familiar brand upon the mount; and he understood many things then, remembering the influx of nesters since his days along the Sombra. Here was a beast broken to the plow and used for a saddle horse as well; farmers often got double duty from their horses; and only a granger would own such an ancient saddle, and only a granger would have a mount that knew no better than to walk away when its reins were dropped.

But he could save some farmer boy a long trudge home, and he led the mount toward the willows and wedged his way through them and came to the bank of the Sombra just as the girl waded ashore and stood naked there before him.

She was like that for a single, long instant, immobilized by astonishment, full-bodied and lovely, the water glistening upon skin brown enough to show that this was not her first stolen swim this summer. She didn't scream, and his fear was that she might. He had a doctor's indifference to nakedness, but this was different; this put a tingle in his skin and brought the blood to the roots of his hair, and he supposed his face must be showing the run of his feelings, and he was sick with a sudden shame, and powerless.

The girl had two choices, and she made her choice quickly. She crossed her arms before her body and darted up the bank, stooping low, and she scooped up a bundle of clothes and plunged headlong into a thicket of brush.

From this cover she said tartly, "You could have called out!"

"I could have called out," he conceded and lowered his glance to the ground and kept it there.

She was making quick movements in the brush. Shortly she emerged, wearing denim trousers and buttoning a cotton shirt over the swell of her breasts. She had brown hair and brown eyes and the kind of face that went with gaily curtained kitchens and flour dough and the smells of baking; but that was only at first glance. Her lips were a little too full, and they made her sensual and roguish at the same time. She clapped a shapeless felt hat upon her head and seated herself upon a rock and began tugging on her boots, and he thought: *Why, I'm more embarrassed than she is!* But he liked this aplomb of hers; she might have been giving him a tongue-lashing for his intrusion, excusing her own carelessness by heaping accusations of carelessness upon him.

He took off his felt slouch hat and ran his fingers through his hair. "I found your horse straying," he said. And then, hoping it would help relieve whatever was left of awkwardness between them, "I'm a doctor. I'm used to the unexpected."

She said, "The next time, you holler."

"I will," he said and put his hat back on and touched the brim of it gravely and turned away.

He had taken five steps before she said, "Just a minute."

He turned, and seeing her again, saw now that there was something familiar about her. She was new here; he was sure of that; she hadn't been part of the buried years, yet the familiarity was there. He said, "Yes?"

"Thanks for fetching back my horse, Doctor."

She was smiling, and her smile was as roguish as he had imagined it would be. It awoke some devil's mood in him; and he said, more gravely than ever, "Perhaps our positions will be reversed some day. Then you can do the same for me."

"I'll be glad to." Her smile never wavered; her eyes were dancing when he put his back to her a second time.

It wasn't until he was into the buggy and had clucked the horse into motion that he realized he hadn't learned her name.

She was of the nester breed; he was sure of that. One of those who came with a heaped wagon to rear a tar-paper covered shack on some desolate quarter section, to break the sod and wring a poor living from it. Her kind was pouring into the West by wagon, by emigrant train, even afoot; they were coming to crowd the range and to make it fruitful and to build the cities and push the frontier into oblivion. They were progress in denim pants; they were the inevitable.

But he was born to cattle, and the sadness at his first sight of Tamerlane today came into him again. An old day ends and the night comes, and there is the ancient promise of another sunrise, but a man remembers only the clearness of yesterday's morning.

Once he looked back; he could see the willows, but the girl and the horse were hidden. He wondered if he would ever see her again, and he carried the thought of her with him until it was banished by the second adventure of this trip from town.

The land had taken to humping its back; and the road, veering away from the river, cut beneath sandy banks and skirted hills too high to climb; and it was in the shadow of one of the cutbanks that he heard the voice. Pain made it feeble; desperation gave it a sharp edge; and it reached into Ives above the clatter of the buggy. The single word, repeated, might have been, "Help!" He didn't know. Again he hauled at the reins and wrapped them around the whipstock and dropped the iron weight; but when he let himself to the ground, he could see no one, and he cried, "Where are you?"

"Up here!" Feebly.

He clawed his way up the sandy face of the cutbank, and he found the man writhing upon its crest, the square-cut man with the brutish shoulders; and there was all of a story here for the reading. Beyond, at the far base of this hill and screened from the road, a saddle horse stood ground-anchored. Not six feet from the man, a rattlesnake lay twitching, but the snake was dead. Cigarette stubs littered the ground around the man, his gun lay at his finger tips—the gun that had killed the snake. But first the snake had struck.

Ives said, "How long ago?" but Brule's answer was a babbling, without meaning.

Ives's instrument case was still in the buggy, but he didn't go after it. He got a jackknife from his pocket and ripped at Brule's right pants leg and exposed the wound; it was in the fleshy part of the calf of his leg, and the leg was swelling. Ives fumbled for a match and held the blade of the knife in the flame, and then bent quickly and made his incisions and put his lips to the wound. He sucked hard and spat, gagging and growing sick. He did this again and again, and after a while he made new incisions at the edge of the swelling. His thought was that all his training hadn't changed the old fundamentals. He'd have handled a rattlesnake bite in just this way ten years ago.

When he was sure he had drawn the poison, he felt Brule's pulse and found it strong. He edged Brule around, wanting the man's body to lie uphill; and a wisp of yellow caught Ives's eye. A bit of paper had worked from Brule's pocket as the man had writhed in pain, and had been concealed by his body. It was the torn half of a hundred-dollar bill, and this Ives thrust back into the man's pocket, understanding now the full story of what had been going on here. Brule groaned, and sanity began to come back into his eyes—sanity and man's oldest fear, for this was the one that had had its start in Eden.

"Am I gonna live, Doc?"

"Likely," Ives said. "You'll have to take it easy for a while, and then I'll get you down to the buggy. I'm going on to Hammer."

Brule said, "If I can travel by buggy, I can travel by horse. I'll make out. I'm not going to Hammer."

Ives shrugged.

"Suit yourself."

Brule said, "What do I owe you for this, Doc?" and it was a sneer.

Ives's lips stiffened. "You don't deal in the kind of coin that interests me. I want you to know I'm not pleased with myself for this. You're a hired killer. In town you were backing up a play for that Lund kid, and I was supposed to be in the middle of it. Now it looks like you're hunting bigger game—hundred-dollar game. Would that be Colonel Carradine?"

Brule's eyes narrowed; viewed this close he was a square-faced man, the blue-black kind who never got a full measure of use from a razor. His lips were lost in stubble, but his teeth showed, yellow and snaggled. He said, "So you found the *dinero?*"

"There was enough sign as it was," Ives said. "Your horse out of sight. An hour's smoking, if a man were keyed up enough to be lighting one after another. The gun. The snake was the thing you didn't count on—the biter got bitten. And of all the men in the world, I had to come along. I should have let you lie. If I'd been more a man and less a doctor, I would have. You weren't worth the bother, Brule."

Brule said, "You talk too much, Doc."

"That's to try to square myself with my own soul. You'll do your waiting another day, on another cutbank. You'll earn the other half of that hundred-dollar bill. And I can remember that I helped kill your man for you, because I could have left you here until the poison worked up to your heart."

Brule said, "Maybe I'll send you a cut when I earn the money." And he grinned.

"Keep it to pay for your own burial," Ives said. "I'll have this to remember—your kind never lives long enough to do any lasting harm. There's always somebody who is faster."

"You better get along, Doc."

"Yes," Ives said, "I'd better get along." And the futility was in him, making him heavy-limbed, the futility of wasted words and wasted effort. Yet the professional in him could not be denied, and he said, without meaning to say it, "You'd better favor that leg for a while. And don't try moving until you are sure you're able."

He turned and clambered down the cutbank to the road; he paused here to beat the dust from his Prince Albert coat, and, this done, he set his foot to the buggy's step. There was fire and sound then, and a motionless moment when the fire and sound engulfed him, and the pain with it, and he had the sensation of being lifted and flung headlong into a vortex of darkness, with time only for one last fleeting thought. Now he knew, too late, for whom it was that Brule had waited by the roadside.

3

Gray Ghost Walking

SHE WAS TEARING MAD AT HIM, AND HE COULDN'T BLAME her. It had been bad enough, busting through the willows and catching her without a stitch of clothes on, and then he'd had to stand there, staring like a schoolboy. She'd used a rock on him, he supposed; his head ached, and he couldn't make his eyes work, and his only real consciousness was of sound. Her voice was a lash laid on him, but there was no coherency to the words, they were just a constant babble, sharp and insistent and perhaps a little desperate. Well, if it made her feel any better to give him a piece of her mind, let her. He wondered why she kept tugging at his armpits.

"You've got to get up!" Suddenly he could make that out clearly. "I can't get you into the buggy, unless you help. You're too heavy!" She said the same thing again, her hands hauling at him.

He got his eyes open then but hastily closed them, the sun was a hammer. But in that brief instant, he glimpsed the sandy face of the cutbank, and the standing buggy, and that was enough to give his memory a prod. This was like one of those nights when you went out on a country call and then headed home in the darkness, stupid for want of sleep. You told yourself you wouldn't sleep, but you did, and then you jarred awake to find your horse nibbling at somebody's haystack fifty miles from nowhere, and you had a first bad moment like this, not finding any reality, and then everything came back.

The girl said, "Don't you understand? I'm trying to help you!"

He remembered Brule then, Brule and the rattlesnake and the torn half of a hundred-dollar bill, and the shot. The girl had got him to a sitting position, and he rolled over to his hands and knees and tried lifting his head, wanting a look at the cutbank for fear Brule was still there waiting to take a second shot. Then he realized that time had passed; the sun had moved. He added this to the sum of his knowledge and concluded that Brule had left him for dead and gone his way and that the girl had come riding along and found him.

She said, "Do you think you could get to your feet?"

He made the try with her tugging at him; he got to a shaky stand and leaned against her; she flung an arm around him and got his left arm across her shoulder. She was supporting most of his weight, and he mumbled something meant to be an apology, and she said, "Just stand like this till you're a little stronger. Then we'll try getting you into the buggy."

He made an impatient gesture with his free hand and took a lurching step toward the buggy. The ground tilted and buckled, and he said crazily, "That's the old years bursting out from underneath." She looked at him, startled, a little scared, and he mustered a smile. He remembered that she wouldn't know about the old years; she hadn't been there. He said, "I'm glad you came along."

He got to the buggy and reached out for it, missing with his first try and then finding a handhold on the top supports. He got his foot on the step, and she pushed at him as he tried hoisting himself upward. He sprawled across the leather-covered seat and might have fallen out the far side, but he reached for a hold on the dashboard. He hoped Marco Stoll's horse wasn't skittish and wouldn't decide to take off at this precise moment, but the horse hadn't run at Brule's shot. He wanted nothing more than to sprawl out on the seat and go to sleep, but the seat was too narrow for that; he'd tried sleeping in a buggy in Oregon when night calls had taken him too far from his office.

The girl seemed to have vanished; he wanted to call out to her, to tell her to come back, but he didn't know her name. Then he heard her voice. She was tying her saddler behind the buggy. She came back into his range of vision, tossing his hat into the buggy and climbing in and tugging at him again, forcing him to a sitting position.

He said, "I'm a hell of a nuisance."

He began exploring his head with his fingers; blood matted his hair, and he deduced that the bullet had raked his scalp, not doing much more than breaking the skin and rendering him unconscious. He thought of Brule and was very angry; Brule had used the devil's own coin to pay his doctor bill. He wondered again if Brule were around but knew there was no use in looking, or in having the girl look. Brule would have used his gun again if he were still in the vicinity.

The girl hoisted the iron weight and set it upon the floorboards. She unwrapped the reins from around the whipstock, and said, "Where to?"

"Hammer," he said.

She turned her head, her eyes startled again, her eyes a

little afraid. She said, "Then you'd be Doctor Ives. I should have figured that out."

He said, "You're one of those nesters, I'd guess. If you're afraid of Hammer, I'll make out alone."

Her eyes became steel. "I'm not afraid of Hammer," she said.

"Good for you!" he said, but it was lost in the clatter of wheels. She had clucked the horse into motion and they were off down the road.

He didn't try talking after that; wheels and hoofs made too much noise; he didn't feel up to the effort of shouting. He thought of trying to bandage his wound, but it had quit bleeding, and he didn't feel up to that effort, either. He watched the girl; she was a good driver; she kept her eyes on the road and her mind on the business, and he liked that. She might have plagued him with a thousand questions; she'd asked none. He appreciated that, too. He couldn't have given the answers, anyway. Brule shot me. Why? Because he was hired to. Who hired him? I don't know. I just don't know, miss. Hell, I haven't been on this range for ten years.

He remembered Cory Lund; the youngster had come to him with a warning and an implied threat, and there was a temper in Cory. But it was not temper but calculated scheming that put a man on a cutbank for patient waiting with a gun. Cory Lund wouldn't have torn a hundred-dollar bill in half. Cory would have done his own gun work; and it pleased Ives to think that he would have seen the color of Cory's eyes at the same time he became aware of Cory's gun. The youngster just didn't have the cut of the back-shooting breed.

He wanted to think this thing through, to reason out why his scalp had had a price on it, but the effort cost him pain, and he gave it up. He had become oblivious to the country through which they passed; he realized that it was mostly up and down, but he no longer looked for familiar landmarks. When he did try to force himself to alertness, he became confused. He would be sure that he remembered a certain rise, and he would be equally sure that the Pritchard place lay just beyond it, and then he'd remember that the Pritchard place was in Oregon. He was slightly delirious and knew it; he would catch the girl looking at him queerly, and he would realize that he'd been babbling aloud and that she'd made no sense out of the words. Always he smiled then.

They came to a fork in the road, and, in a moment of lucidity, he remembered the fork. The main road led straight on north to Hammer; the road to the left veered westward to the upper Sombra. Once this second road had been no more than a shadow upon the grass; now it was worn as deep as Hammer's road, and he supposed this was the way the nesters went on their comings and goings from Tamerlane. The girl hesitated at the fork, but only for a second. The buggy rolled on northward.

Again he said, "Good for you!"

They should be at Hammer's gate within the hour, he judged, and then he forgot about it, losing himself in that half-world of pain and fever, and beginning to babble again. The girl was keeping the horse at a good lively clip; her glance, when it was directed at him, grew more worried. It seemed increasingly harder for him to sit up; he wanted to explore his wound again to see if it had started bleeding once more, but he didn't want to take his hands from the dashboard and the top supports. After a while he saw the dying sunlight glinting on barbed wire, and Hammer's gate was ahead. It was a wooden gate with a rustic arch above it, made from peeled willows, with the word *Hammer* shaped upon it.

The girl said, "We're nearly there."

He giggled. "Hammer," he said. "They should have

added Dante's line: 'All hope abandon, ye who enter here.' "

She started to dismount to open the gate; some instinct of gallantry made him try to struggle out of the buggy. She pushed him back firmly, saying nothing. When she climbed in and drove through, he wondered dazedly why she drove twice the length of the buggy before getting out to close the gate. Then he remembered that her saddle horse was trailing behind the buggy.

Now they were winding along a remembered avenue of cottonwoods; Colonel Carradine long ago had planted these trees beside the road reaching to his ranch house, and Ives wondered at the quirk that had made a man from the treeless Texas plains plant shade trees in the equally treeless country of eastern Montana. The shadows lay long, flickering hourglasses for a dying day. And then the ranch buildings sprawled ahead—the long, low ranch house, the barn and outhouses and corrals; and the buggy wheeled into the space before the ranch house and came to a stop.

A dog came running to greet them; Ives didn't remember this dog. He had expected to see part of the crew in the yard, but the crew wasn't here; there was just the one old man sanding before the ranch-house gallery, the wild-maned old man in the tattered clothes, and the girl on the gallery. The girl was tall and black-haired and wore a long trailing dress with a bustle, and she was shading her eyes with one hand and peering at the buggy as if trying to see whom it held. Ives didn't remember the girl, either, not at first. And then he said, wonderingly, "Montana!"

Even then, she didn't make sense to him, until he began figuring. He'd been fifteen when he'd left; that made him twenty-five now. Tana had been thirteen; he put his mind to subtracting and adding and began giggling at the swirling figures. Shucks, he was doing it the hard way! Thirteen and ten made Tana twenty-three and a woman.

The girl at the reins said sharply, "Well, come and help me with him!"

Tana came running down the steps and across to the buggy; Ives tried rising to meet her and almost pitched to the ground. Tana got hold of him, and the nester girl's hands were under his armpits again, and between them they managed to get him unloaded. Tana cried, "Tom! Come here and lend me a hand!"

The old fellow with the wild tangle of hair came forward, his laughter a dry cackle, and he said, "So the grave give him up. I always said it would. You recollect, I always said it would."

Ives thought; *Why, it's old Tom Feather, and just as crazy as ever!* Tana had an arm around him, and he tried to smile at her; her face was close to his and he saw that she'd become a very handsome woman. One couldn't call her pretty; her perfection of feature wasn't of that kind. He'd remembered her as a tall girl, given to quiet ways and quiet speech; the years had made her graver.

Between the two, Tana and Tom Feather, they got him up the gallery steps; he wondered about the nester girl, he struggled to turn and look for her, and he saw her untying her horse from the back of the buggy and mounting the animal. He wanted to call after her, to tell her to wait so he could thank her properly for what she'd done for him. He made the try, but it was only a croak.

Tana called to the girl.

"I think he wants you to wait."

The girl turned in her saddle, her face wooden. "I've got him here," she said. "He can tell you all you'll need to know. Tell Colonel Carradine I wouldn't have set foot on Hammer for my own sake."

Tana said, "I want you to know I'm grateful. And that the colonel will be grateful, too."

But the nester girl was wheeling her horse and lifting it to a gallop, and soon she was lost in the cottonwoods, and Tana said, "Come, Brian. We've got to get you to bed."

They half dragged him through the house, and he saw the cool whiteness of a bed in a dim room, and it was the easiest thing in the world to fall upon that bed. Tana tugged at his boots, and he heard her say, "Get his clothes off him, Tom, and get him under the covers. I'll heat some water."

Ives said, "I never even found out her name!"

"She's Marybelle Lund," Tana said. "She's new here since your time, Brian."

"Lund—" he repeated, wondering where he'd heard the name, and then it came back to him. Lund—Cory Lund—and he knew now why the girl had looked familiar when he'd first seen her. He began to laugh; it seemed funnier than all get-out. Cory Lund's sister!

Tom Feather was fumbling with Ives's coat, and Tana was gone from the room, and Feather was babbling away about something as he worked, but Ives could make no sense out of it. He reflected that that was probably how he'd sounded to Marybelle Lund, and he wondered which of them was the crazier, himself or Tom Feather.

He was under the covers when Tana came back into the room; she seated herself by the bed and began swabbing at his wound, and he noticed that every movement of hers was precise; she carried her own kind of serenity into all her actions.

He said, "My instrument case is out in the buggy, but I don't think I'm up to sewing myself up. Clean it up, and I'll show you how to bandage it."

When the job was done, Tana turned to Tom Feather.

"Tom, you'd better go find the colonel and tell him about this. Can you remember?"

Feather's laugh was that familiar dry cackle. "I'll remember, and he'll remember," he said. "Oh, it will be a great day for the colonel!"

He was gone then, and Tana stood beside the bed and said, "Do you suppose you could eat something, Brian?"

He said, "I'll sleep. I'll feel better then."

She looked down upon him and the serenity fled from her and she leaned and put her hands upon his naked shoulders. He couldn't remember her ever having been this close to him before. "Brian," she said, "what a way for you to come home!"

He said, "What the devil is happening on this range?"

"You mustn't talk now," she said. "Wait till after the colonel comes."

Three times now she'd referred to her grandfather and always she'd called him the colonel as though there were no personal tie between them. She might have been a hand drawing Hammer's pay. That was queer, he thought, and he tried to remember if she'd always talked that way, or if she'd had another name for the colonel in the old days. He couldn't remember and the task seemed hardly worth the bother, and it was much easier to slip into troubled sleep.

Sometimes he awoke. Night had claimed the room, and Tana was there and Tana was gone and Tana was there again; only sometimes she wasn't Tana, she was Marybelle Lund, but that didn't make sense, for Marybelle Lund hadn't stepped into Hammer's ranch house. Marco Stoll didn't have any right being here, either, hovering over his bed, nor did his old schoolteacher with her crazy jingle about, "When I was going to St. Ives—"

There was no reality to any of them, and when the gray ghost of a man paced the room and looked down upon him, the old scar standing white upon his forehead, Ives didn't try to call his name, not being sure whether Colonel Carradine was real or made of the stuff of feverish dreams.

4

Man with a Star

ONCE MONTANA HAD KNOWN AN AUTUMN WHEN THE wild geese had wedged southward early, and the range cattle had taken on a heavier, shaggier coat of hair, and white Arctic owls had come to the range, and the Indians had drawn their blankets closer, remembering some terrible experience of the past. Storm came, and cold, the endless months of it, and the spring found the coulees and draws strewed with the carcasses of cattle, and the day of the longhorn had passed. The hard lesson had been learned. Blooded cattle came to the ranges, for if a man concentrated on quality in his beef, rather than quantity, he could provide feed and weather his herds through such winters. Thus had the new day come about, and it brought a new breed of cattle and cattlemen; but there were the old kings still, grown sadder and wiser.

They were of a breed that was Texas-born, those giants of the saddle, and their roots had known Tennessee, and Scotland, perhaps, and they were the kind who had a taste for feuding in their blood, and a quick eye along the barrel of a squirrel rifle, and a touch of whang leather in their souls. The treeless llanos of Texas had known them. The streets of Dodge had echoed to their roistering. Powder River had caught their bearded reflection when the herds were first turned northward to the new graze of Montana. They were unreconstructed Rebels, given to old clothes, even when prosperity was upon them, given to an easy way with their men; and they had the look of too many hours in the saddle. They were a type, and no one winter could blot them out. But sometimes they were individuals, and then you had a Colonel Kevin Carradine.

Looking at him, Brian Ives thought of these things, and he thought, too, of the monk named Mendel who had certain theories about heredity, and he wondered how one went about accounting for a Colonel Carradine.

Carradine was of the South, but in his lean lankiness and thin, blue-veined hands and finely chiseled aristocratic features there was the remembrance of a different south than Texas's, a malarial south of swamp and moss-veiled trees and great white houses with fluted pillars. True, he was an unreconstructed Rebel; he was all Texan in that respect. His title was more than honorary—he had followed Beauregard through the years of the war—but he affected the white goatee and mustache of a Kentucky judge of horses and whisky. There was little of cattledom about him. He had spent a lot of his life in a saddle, but his walk didn't show it. He dressed as though every day were Sunday; he favored black suits and black string ties and hats that would have needed only the insignia to be Confederate campaign hats. Your cattle king is salty of speech, and a sprinkle of Spanish is on his tongue. Colonel Carradine's house held more books than one man could have read in a lifetime, but he had read them, and you knew it when he talked.

He was not talking today, not yet. He sat on Hammer's gallery; and Brian Ives sat beside him, nearly a whole man after his night of tossing and turning; and they looked out toward the avenue of cottonwoods and held their silence, but there was no communion in it, only an awkwardness. At table an hour before, Carradine had been frigidly polite. Now he might have been a man who was waiting. At last he said, "What brought you back to us, sir?"

The "sir" was the surprising thing; perhaps it was a concession to Ives's maturity; perhaps it was a closing out of older days when they had been father and son, after a queer fashion. Ives had had no chance to talk with Tana, and because of this he was careful with his answer, wanting it to hold no commitment, and he said, "Call it homesickness, if you like."

Carradine turned his face toward Ives. He was an ashy-skinned man whom the sun had never touched; he looked like ice, but in his eyes, blue and level beneath tufted brows, Ives had always seen a banked fire. The colonel said, "I took the liberty of having one of my crew return the horse and buggy to town this morning. Marco Stoll knows he is not welcome on this ranch, in any form or manner!"

"He intimated as much," Ives said. "But I was grateful for the buggy."

"It was his way of jibing at me," Carradine said emphatically. "I grant your innocence in the matter." He dismissed the subject with a wave of his hand. "Perhaps you intend to start a practice here. The Aesculapian art died on this range when Doctor Ellenberg died."

Anger stirred in Ives. He had got money from this man in the years of his study, but never had there been a letter, never had there been the slightest interest in his work or his plans or his future. The day he had got his diploma, there had been a present—a meerschaum pipe of all things—and Ives had never used it. But he remembered the money, and he kept his voice civil. "It might not be a bad idea. The country is filling up."

The scar on Carradine's forehead turned a slight pink. "That might be changed."

Ives said bluntly, "You mean that you intend to run the nesters off the range."

"You're a doctor," Carradine said. "Do you lance an abscess or poultice it?"

"I do whatever any individual case dictates. A parable would be pointless. I'm told that you intend importing gunmen. I don't think I need to tell you that you'll be writing your own doom if you do."

Carradine's eyebrows arched. "Whoever your informant was, he seems to know a great deal about my affairs. You've evaded my question, sir. Are you going into practice here?"

"I haven't decided," Ives said. "Would I have any patients? Or would they all remember that I'm tied to Hammer? I've stopped a bullet since I came home. I suppose that's a sign of the times."

Carradine said, "That makes me obligated to you. From what Montana tells me, the bullet was likely intended for me. Will you inform me how I can discharge the debt as quickly and as thoroughly as possible?"

Ives thought: *You might give me a civil word, and that would do!* But he said nothing. Around him Hammer dozed in the afternoon's heat; some of the crew stirred about bunkhouse and corrals; they had ridden in last night with the colonel, Ives judged, fetched by crazy Tom Feather. Some of the older hands had come to the gallery to shake his hand and pay their respects, but the colonel had been there beside him, so they had made this ritual brief, giving a hollow tone to it. Tom Feather had not been among them. Ives would have liked a few words with Feather.

Feather had thought him a man risen from the dead yesterday; he wanted to know more about that.

Tana was in the house. Ives was conscious of her movement; he wondered if she was listening now, and because she might be, he said, "I hope you'll call off this notion of warring against the nesters."

The colonel said, "Should it matter to you?"

"I don't know," Ives said. "Each of us has got to think according to his light. I used to suppose that a doctor was some kind of miracle man; I've lived to learn that his knowledge isn't as omniscient as people like to think. I've ridden thirty miles through an Oregon blizzard to sit by a bedside where I knew I couldn't do any earthly good. But maybe I made some poor devil's last hours a little more comfortable, and maybe I brought a measure of faith to the people he left behind him. We can't stop suffering, but it's been kind of worked into my grain to lessen human suffering as much as I can. And that can't be done with imported gunmen."

He expected the colonel's sneer, and he expected the colonel's derision, and they might have goaded him to speaking a fuller truth; they might have made him say that he had become a doctor because the colonel, in other days, had made him feel unwanted and useless; and he might have said, too, that an antagonism had been born in those days that made it natural now to pit himself against anything that was of the colonel's planning. But the colonel didn't sneer; perhaps the years had brought him that much tolerance. He only nodded.

"Certainly we must think according to our light! Mine is a more practical one. I came north to this range. I brought my cattle here and wintered them through a hard winter and saw myself ruined, so I started over. I claimed this land and salted it down with my sweat to prove my claim. Now barbed wire has been strung upon it and corn fields shut me out from a river I've always owned, and my beef goes into nester frying pans. The law says the nester has a right to be here, and the courts move almighty slow. A gun works faster. I've always fought for what is mine. I always will."

Ives said hotly, "Then go ahead and fight. And before the year is out, they'll be planting wheat over your grave."

"Perhaps," the colonel said.

He eased back into his chair, suddenly become an old, tired man; and there was born in Ives a first sympathy and a new respect that were tempered by the old remembrances. Then he saw Carradine sit bolt upright, the man's lanky body stiffening and his face grown stern again; and Ives looked and saw the man riding up through the avenue of cottonwoods to the very yard of Hammer.

Carradine said softly, "The nerve! The unmitigated nerve of him!"

The man was dismounting; he was a young man, and he wore the hated denim of the sodbusters, but he also wore a calfskin vest, and a ball-pointed sheriff's star was pinned upon it. He came toward the gallery with a loose-jointed stride, he was tall and long of arm and leg and boyish of face, with a bridge of freckles across his nose. There was a certain bravado in his utter carelessness; if fear was in him, it lay buried deep. He said, very casually, "Good afternoon, Colonel."

Carradine said, "Can it be, sir, that you didn't understand me the last time we met?"

The sheriff shrugged. "This isn't a pleasure jaunt. I wouldn't have set foot on Hammer if I didn't have to." He looked at Ives. "You'd be the doctor?"

"I'm Brian Ives," Ives said.

"I'm sorry," the sheriff said. "You'll have to ride to town with me. I'm Rod Benedict, sheriff of the county."

"For what reason?" Carradine demanded.

"For arrest on suspicion of murder," Benedict said. "He had a run-in with young Cory Lund yesterday. Cory hasn't been seen since. This morning his horse was found standing at his corral gate. With blood on the saddle. I'm sorry, but you see how it looks."

Carradine came to his feet, the banked fire blazing in his eyes; but Ives thrust out his arm, the gesture holding the colonel silent.

Ives said, "I can account for my movements, Sheriff. I left town not long after I saw Lund. I met two people on the road to Hammer. One of them came the last half of the trip with me."

"I know about that, Doctor," Benedict said. "Marybelle told me. But you were alone for quite a spell. Supposing Cory cut out of town ahead of you and waited along the road to take up where he'd left off. Supposing one word had led to another, and you hadn't had any choice. You see how it could have been?"

Men were drifting into the front yard, the men of Hammer who weren't in saddles today. The colonel hadn't raised his voice, but they were here. They stood in little knots of twos and threes; they stood slaunchwise, their thumbs hooked in their gun belts; they stood, saying nothing, but they were here. Ives could feel them as well as see them, and the makings of big trouble were in the air. The color fled from Benedict's face; his freckles stood out; and in the frozen look of him Ives read Benedict's awareness that only a signal was needed now.

The signal would have to come from the colonel. Benedict's eyes did not leave the colonel's face. Then Carradine said, "You can go back to the farmers who put you in office and tell them that this insult to Hammer failed. Tell them you haven't grown wide enough across the britches to pluck a prisoner off Hammer."

Skirts swished softly, and this was how Ives knew that

Tana had come to the porch. He turned his head only slightly; the grouped men in the yard had a mesmerizing effect on him, but he saw Tana out of a corner of his eye; he saw her standing rigid, a ghost of a woman, and he saw what leaped into Benedict's eyes, the hunger and the glory; and he knew, suddenly, the real reason why Colonel Carradine had forbidden this man to set foot upon Hammer.

Benedict said slowly, "I'm not going back without him, Colonel," and he reached for his holstered gun and drew it, the movement deliberately awkward and slow. Any man in that yard could have beaten him, but the signal hadn't come from the colonel.

Carradine said, "You realize, sir, that you'd get no farther than the gate?"

Tana drew in her breath, the sound like a sob. "Rod! No!" she cried.

Benedict shook his head; Ives wondered if this was a display of stubborness or courage. "I'm not going back without him," Benedict said. "I don't say he's guilty; that's for somebody else to decide. But he's under arrest."

Ives said quietly, "I'll go along with you, Benedict."

The colonel's blue eyes moved from Benedict, touching Ives. The colonel said, "Have you no more brains than to insult me when I'm trying to protect you? Don't you see what this will mean to Hammer prestige? They don't care about you one way or the other. But every farmer along the Sombra will gloat tonight, telling how one of their breed came to Hammer and walked away with you."

Ives said again, "I'll go along with you, Benedict."

Tana said quickly, "You'll want your things. I'll get them for you." She darted into the house, and Ives turned and followed her. He met her returning from the bedroom, the carpetbag in one hand, his instrument case in the other. He hadn't meant to take the instrument case along; the carpetbag held clean shirts and he might need a change, but he took both bags. In the semigloom of the house, Tana's face was a white shadow.

Ives said softly, "Don't worry. No harm will come to him."

She pressed his arm. She said, "Thanks, Brian."

He said, "I'll clear this up in a hurry. We'll have our chance to talk then."

He came out upon the gallery; Colonel Carradine still stood, and Rod Benedict hadn't moved in the yard, and Hammer's crew waited. Ives went down the gallery steps, not looking at the colonel, and he said to Benedict, "Will your horse carry double? I haven't a mount of my own."

Benedict grinned then, and, grinning, pouched his gun. "I reckon," he said. "Here, I'll tie those bags to the saddle."

Only when Ives had swung up behind the man did he look back at the colonel; Carradine had sat down in the chair, and he was a man turned to stone, and long after Ives had looked away, he felt the colonel's gaze upon him, he felt the colonel pulling at him and trying to hold him here.

5

Behind Bars

THEY RODE IN SILENCE AT FIRST; AND WHILE THEY WERE within gunshot of Hammer, rigidity held Rod Benedict, and Ives could feel the tension in the man and knew then how deeply fear had driven into Benedict and how well he had concealed it in Hammer's yard. This gave him the measure of Benedict; only an idiot is ever completely unafraid. He thought to himself that here was quite a man, and he felt drawn to Benedict, and he tasted the irony of this. Benedict had come to Hammer to arrest him, and now Ives was Benedict's friend. He was even proving his friendship; he was covering Benedict's back.

Beyond the fence with its arched gateway, Benedict slouched in his saddle, but there was a constant alertness in the man. They jogged on; they came in due course to the cutbank where Ives had fallen beneath Brule's gun, and Benedict gave this cutbank more than a passing glance, and Ives remembered that the sheriff had talked to Marybelle Lund. He remembered, too, that Marybelle was Cory's sister, and he broke the silence to ask, "What does the girl think? Does she think I shot her brother?"

Over his shoulder, Benedict said, "Nobody's ever known what Marybelle thought about anything." Then: "Who was it cut you down yesterday, Doc? Did Cory Lund get in one good lick?"

"The fellow calls himself Brule."

Benedict considered this for a reflective moment. "That makes more sense. Brule, eh? He hasn't showed himself since yesterday."

Ives said, "I got a mighty sore head out of the deal. Would you mind either keeping this cayuse at a gallop or holding him to a walk?"

Benedict said, "Hell, I never thought about that! Sorry, Doc. Could you use a drink of water?"

They left the road and angled overland to the Sombra and rested the horse among the willows. There was a droning peace here today; the river made placid sounds and ran a quiet course through this stretch of country, and sunlight danced upon the river's surface. Ives had his drink and looked upon the water and found himself wondering for the first time how it had come by its name. Texas men had dubbed it, of course. They had brought the language of *mañana*-land to these latitudes and fastened it carelessly upon many things. *Sombra*—It meant shade and shadow and spirit and ghost, as he remembered the word; he thought of Colonel Carradine; here was the ghost of Carradine's dead hopes. But the word also meant shelter, protection; and he thought of the nesters who had broken the ground beside this water.

He looked at Benedict and said, "How long have you known Tana Carradine?"

Something closed down behind Benedict's eyes, shutting out the friendliness, shutting out the intimacy. "It doesn't matter," he said.

Ives made his apology with a nod of his bandaged head. "You puzzle me, friend. Farmer votes may have pinned that star on you. But I'll bet the dust you've tasted was the dust of the drag, not of the plow."

Benedict's grin came back, and the curtain lifted behind his eyes. "Can't a cowboy hanker to put down roots?"

"With a star on his vest?"

"I worked for Carradine," Benedict said. "That was long after you left the ranch. The cattlemen had prempted the land; you know that. To make it legal under the Homestead Act they had their men, and each new man who came, file on a hundred and sixty acres each, and they threw up shacks for them so they could qualify. The thought came to me one dark night, since I was going through the motions of being a homesteader, why shouldn't I end up by owning the land?"

Ives smiled. "How long did it take the colonel to hand you your walking-papers after that?"

"I disrecollect. He was a powerfully angry man, when I told him. But maybe he was right, at that. I raised the sickest damn corn you ever did see. But the farmers knew which side I was on. Come last election, they wrote me into the ballot. They tell me the colonel didn't eat for three days."

Ives looked at the sun. "We'd better be getting on into town."

They rode into Tamerlane at dusk, and they spread excitement before them as they came down the street. Ives saw men stare and then turn and run to carry the news to others, and the word was a rock dropped into water and spreading out ever widening circles. Marco Stoll sat at his window, and Ives gave him a wave. Stoll nodded back; he looked like man far too surprised for coherent thinking.

The jailhouse sat on the town's edge, but Benedict had passed it on entering; he rode to the far end of the single street and dismounted before a small frame house and let Ives into the yard and into the kitchen of the house.

Benedict called out, "Maw!" A woman materialized from somewhere in the house; she had the long legs and long arms of her son, but there was a prim severity to her. Benedict said, "My mother. She's Kansas folks. When I became a landowner, I sent for her. That was part of the notion. Now she keeps the victuals warm when I go on long rides." He grinned at the woman. "Could you rustle up some supper for us, Maw? And you might shake out the sheets on that spare bed. This is Doc Ives. He may be here quite a few days."

Ives said, "You mean to keep me here? In this house?"

"The jail isn't the best in the world, Doc."

Ives said, "If it had been me that had turned up missing, and Cory Lund you had to collar, where would you have put him?"

"In the jail, I guess."

"Then that's where I'm going."

Benedict spread his hands. "Hell, Doc, I might not have ridden away from Hammer with a whole skin today. Don't you think I know that?"

Ives said, "That doesn't matter. There's likely to be trouble enough on this range without hurrying it. What are your farmers going to say if you pamper me?" He stepped toward the door. "Do I have to lock myself up?"

Benedict said slowly, "Maybe you're right. Maybe you're right at that."

His mother said in a passionless voice, "Of course he's right."

They left the house and climbed on the horse again and rode back to the jail; grouped men watched their passing, holding silent; but the feel of them was in the air. And now Ives knew how Benedict had felt in Hammer's yard when only the signal had been needed.

The rigidity came back into Benedict, and he might have been talking to himself. He said, "Don't let it worry you.

Nobody's ever tried to take a prisoner away from me. But they liked Cory a lot; you've got to know that. They liked him a lot."

Before the jail building, Benedict untied Ives's bags from the saddle and fetched them into the office and placed them on his desk. Behind this room was another, the single cell of the jail, its barred door ajar. When Ives walked into the cell, Benedict said, "I'll go fetch you some supper. Just make yourself at home." He hesitated, looking toward his desk where a huge key lay. "If you would just give me your word—"

"Lock me up," Ives said.

Benedict shut the barred door and turned the key in the lock and put the key back on his desk, and Ives watched him walk across the office and close the outer door behind him quietly. Within half an hour, Benedict was back, bearing a tray. He watched while Ives ate, standing with his shoulders against the cell wall, thoughtful and somber and grown graver since Ives had last seen him.

Benedict said, "I'll be moseying around the town, Doc. If you want anything, set up a holler. Somebody will hear you. Send him for me."

"I'll make out."

Again the door was locked, and Ives seated himself on the cot, which, with washbowl and stand, was the only furnishing of the cell. The night was coming down; a grayness invaded the cell and made its corners murky, and beyond the single barred window the sounds of the town rose, formless and without meaning. But Ives was remembering those quiet groups who had watched his passage.

An hour passed before he heard boots in the office again; it was too dark to see who had entered, but it was not Benedict; Ives had learned to recognize the sheriff's walk. The man fumbled about; a match flared and was touched to the wick of a lamp on Benedict's desk, and then the man stepped to the barred door and thus, standing between the lamp and Ives, he was in gaunt silhouette, a big, broad-shouldered man. He said with just a trace of Scandinavian accent, "You're Doc Ives?"

"Yes," he said. "I'm Ives."

"I'm Elisha Lund."

Only the barred door was between them, and the key was there on the desk. Ives thought: *Did he leave the key lying around so anybody could pick it up and pay me a visit?* And then he understood. That was exactly what Rod Benedict had done, but the key was for Hammer if Hammer came to try a jail-delivery. The key was to make it easy. Each man paid his debts in his own coin—the Brules and the Rod Benedicts.

But no one had counted on Elisha Lund.

He stood there at the door, his huge hands fastened upon the bars; Ives saw the yellow beard, and the gaunt, hard-planed features; here was a Viking long divorced from the seas, a rover who had taken to tilling the soil and learned a measure of peace, a measure of tolerance from the transformation. His breed had scarred the dirt of Minnesota and the Dakotas, looking always westward, and with a wagon and a pot and a pan had defied cattledom. But this one was an individual, and his son's horse had come home with blood on its saddle, and Ives eased nearer to the edge of the cot and planted his feet solidly on the floor.

Lund said, "I just"—it sounded a little like "yoost"—"wanted a look at you."

"Take your look," Ives said with neither resignation nor truculence.

Lund peered at him; he shook his giant's head then. "You didn't do it," he said. "You ain't a killer."

Startled, Ives said, "How can you be sure? Any man can be pushed too far."

"You wouldn't have let yourself be brought in and locked up. You wouldn't have risked that. You are a goot man, I think. My son is wild; he was born to trouble. But he wouldn't have got bad trouble from you."

"He ordered me out of town."

Lund's huge shoulders lifted, fell. "As long as Colonel Carradine lives, our people will know not peace but a sword. My son had heard of you. You was one more gun on the side of the Hammer. He did what he thought best. Now he is dead. But you didn't do it."

Ives said, "I hope the other farmers see it that way."

Lund said very somberly, "I hope so, too."

He turned away, and Ives said, "You don't want the six-guns banging along the Sombra. Neither do I. However all this turns out, I want you to remember that."

Lund nodded. "Yes."

Here was a man who had come on his own special business, and, having finished that business, he wasn't going to tarry. Ives judged that that sort of directness would mark all of Lund's actions, and he said nothing further to stay the man. Lund crossed to the desk; Ives heard the whoosh of the man's breath as he extinguished the lamp. The outer door opened and closed. Ives sank back upon the cot, and it was then his name was whispered at the cell's window. He walked to the bars and peered out and saw dimly the full-moon face of Marco Stoll.

Stoll said, "I've been waiting here till that old fool left. I heard what he said."

Ives said, "I think he meant it."

One of Stoll's pudgy hands flickered whitely in the darkness, a gesture of dismissal. "He couldn't stop a pack if it came howling for you. There's a lot of talk in town tonight. Cory was well liked. I've come to tell you to get set for a run. I'll fetch you a horse as soon as I can sneak one out of the livery stable."

"The talk's ugly?" Ives asked.

"Very ugly."

For a moment the fear strangled Ives, the sudden, rising, consuming fear, the fear of a man who knows what the combined anger of many men can do. Then he said, "No."

Stoll said, "Are you crazy?"

"Lund's on my side. And Benedict. They'll talk the rest out of anything foolish."

"You can be safe on Hammer when they do the talking."

"No," Ives said again.

Stoll held silent for a moment. Then he said, "Would you mind telling my why?"

"Supposing a mob comes and finds this jail empty, Stoll. They'll be up into saddles and riding for Hammer, won't they? Some little thing like that will set off the fireworks. And what will it add up to but a bunch of dead men?"

Stoll said, "This is a poor time to play noble!"

"It's not that," Ives said. "I'm scared—scared as hell. But I didn't need to come here. Now that I'm here, I'd undo what I've done if I cut and ran."

Stoll gave this his consideration. "Perhaps you're right," he said. "But remember this—there'll be three against them. Benedict and Elisha Lund. And me."

"Thanks," Ives said, and Stoll began to fade back into the shadows. "And thanks, too," Ives called softly, "for that horse you intended bringing."

Stoll called back, "I'll keep an eye on things."

Ives went to the cot again and seated himself and let time slip away; the darkness deepened; beyond the cell window, it grew to blank out what little there had been to see; but the sounds were still there. The sounds were beyond translation, and the feat mounted in him and he began wondering if he were a fool not to have heeded Stoll; he began wondering if he could call to somebody and send word to the man. And then the fatalism of his profession crept into him and brought him peace. This was like sitting beside a sickbed; a man did what he could and waited the long night out, and the rest of it was beyond his power.

Footsteps were in the office again.

One person. His first hope was that it was Rod Benedict, but he knew instantly that it wasn't the sheriff; the steps were too light; the steps were a woman's. She was groping about the desk; the key rattled in the lock and the door opened, and he expected her to be Tana; Tana owed him something, too.

Marybelle Lund said, "Doc?"

"Here," he said. He could make out her face dimly, but it was her voice that told him how strong was the excitement that held her.

She said, "Thank heavens for a careless sheriff. The key was on his desk, big as life. And your bags are out here, too. I've got a horse for you."

The humor of this struck him, and he said, "This is the damnedest jail to get into and stay in that I've ever heard of. Everybody wants me free. Everybody but me."

She said, "I've found Cory."

He came to his feet. "Alive?"

"Up in the Sombra Hills. He needs a doctor. Come on,now."

He crossed the cell. "I'll have to find Benedict first."

She said angrily, "There's no time! Cory's unconscious—shot. Maybe he'll die."

He fumbled in the office's darkness and got his hands on his instrument case and carpetbag. He said, "Do you suppose there's pencil and paper around here? I'll leave a note for him."

She said, "Can't you understand that every second may

count? What good will a note do? Bring Cory back to Benedict. That will make more sense than any note. Please, oh, please hurry!"

He said, "All right."

When they stepped out the front door and he saw the two waiting saddle horses, he hesitated, but only for a second. He was remembering Marco Stoll, who had also been willing to provide a horse; he was remembering that he refused Stoll. What was the difference in running away with the help of one person or another? Tamerlane's people would read his absence each with his own eyes. Then he thought of Cory Lund, and the instrument case grew heavy in his hands, for he was thinking, again, that here was another time when it might be better to be more a man and less a doctor. But he hoisted the case to a saddle and hoisted himself into the saddle and put his back to the jail.

6

Feather's Place

MARYBELLE LED THE WAY OUT OF TAMERLANE; THEY clattered into the darkness quickly and thereafter the night was their cloak, and this escape had been so woefully easy that Ives wondered again if Rod Benedict had made it so. They were pointed due north, not taking any of the roads, and Ives worried about gopher holes; but when he tried speaking of this to the girl, they were moving too fast, and the words were jammed back in his mouth. He sensed soon that they were skirting the Sombra; he could see the marching willows dimly, but all the land was different by night; it was shapeless and lighted only by starshine, and its vastness was something that waited beyond the fringe of perception to pounce upon them.

Reluctance was still in Ives; every instinct told him that this was no way to quit Tamerlane, not when all the factors were considered, and he looked back often until even the lights were lost. And then, because a sound reached through the clatter of hoofs to touch him, he reined short and stood up in his stirrups, listening. Marybelle wheeled her horse about and said impatiently, "What is it?"

"Gunfire," he said, but he wasn't sure. "Back in town. What do you suppose has cut loose? Maybe we should go and see about it."

Her face in the starshine had none of the roguishness, the sensuality. She might have been his mother and he a recalcitrant child. Sternness drew her lips firm, and her eyes had the same chill he'd seen in Cory Lund's in Tamerlane. She said, "Is he to die while we ride around in circles?"

He listened hard for the sound; he thought he heard it again, but it was only the ghost of sound; it defied capture like a handful of smoke. He shrugged. "Perhaps you're right."

She said peremptorily, "Come along," not waiting for his acquiescence; and he wondered if her wilfulness was made of the moment or if it lay deep within her always, needing only something like this to bring it forth. He thought to himself that her man would never have to worry about the decisions; she would make them for him. Yet her steel might be the saving of Cory Lund, and he had to admire it. He could remember no woman who had ever been really concerned about Brian Ives, and for a moment he was jealous.

They rode onward; to Ives it became a blind game of follow-the-leader; he was vaguely conscious of the river to his left and the high lift of the hills ahead, but the world had really narrowed to the horse and rider before him. Starshine reflected from the mount's glossy rump. Sometimes he tried to get stirrup to stirrup with Marybelle, but he found this futile. No words passed between them; there was no time for words. He wanted to ask the exact nature of Cory's wound, but he let this wait

After hours he saw lights twinkling, the yellow pinpoints of kerosene lamps in unshaded windows; and this surprised him. He raked up all his memories of this land

and couldn't account for the lights; by his calculations Hammer lay almost due east of them now, and the other cattle ranches were across the river. Then he remembered the homesteaders and realized he and Marybelle were flanking the settlement that had grown along the upper Sombra. A dog barked at them, and the sound held a strange comfort. The night lost its vastness and its mystery; people were near.

Once they rested their horses so close to a tar-paper shack that Ives could see into the window. A gaunt man passed back and forth, lost to sight and appearing again, like some mechanical man, wound up and set to this definite to-and-fro motion. Some instinct of his profession gave Ives an answer to the riddle of the sleepless man. There was sickness here; there was a shadow upon the shack. He asked a question.

"This is Jensen's place," Marybelle said. "Their child's been ailing."

They lifted to a gallop again. They passed other shacks; there was a likeness to them, each was blank with the blight of poverty, each was a monument to dogged perseverance; and Ives found mockery in the thought that such flimsiness was the stronghold against which Colonel Carradine pitted himself. Soon they had to slow to a walk; they had left the homesteads behind, and the way was lifting upward, and stunted trees began to show themselves, and then they were into deeper timber. Sometimes they had to dismount and lead their horses. Ives shifted his balance to the stars and was surprised to find it no later than it was.

Marybelle said, "It's not much farther."

The shack lay back in screening timber, and they didn't see the light until they were almost upon the place; and Marybelle, back in her saddle again, reined short then and reached her hand to Ives's arm. She said, "I left no light!"

and fear was in her voice, and a need for him. This was comforting, for suddenly she was a woman after all, and she was leaning upon him.

He said, "Why, this is Tom Feather's place. The old coot is probably here."

Still the fear was in her. "I wish we had a gun," she said.

"Tom wouldn't hurt a fly," he told her and jogged his horse forward.

He remembered this place; it was made of logs and was sod-roofed, and it was as old as Hammer. Carradine sometimes used it as a line shack, but at this season it stood empty except when Tom Feather chose to hole up here. Sometimes Feather fancied himself a prospector, and this was the base of his operations along the little streams that fed the Sombra. At least it had been that way in the old days. Ives drew up in the stump-strewn clearing before the place and called tentatively, "Tom?"

Lamplight made a rectangle when the door opened; against the light Tom stood, his wild eyes peering out from his wild tangle of whiskers like a beast's in a thicket. He shaded his eyes with both hands and said, placidly, "Oh, it's you, Jim. Come in. Come in, boy." Then, cautiously: "Who's that with you, Jim?"

"A friend," Ives said. "You got a sick fellow here, Tom?"

"He stopped lead," Feather said. "Always it's guns, eh, Jim?" Fear took hold of him and he was a man about to run to cover; he crouched, looking to right and left. "You won't let them gun down Tom? You won't let them, will you, Jim?"

Ives said, "Of course not," the one word beating steadily through his brain. *Jim—Jim—*Feather had never called him by that name, not in all the years.

Marybelle was tying her horse to a bush. She came

forward into the light; Ives took her by the elbow and steered her to the doorway, Feather falling back to let them enter. The one room of the shack held a rusty stove, two rickety chairs, a table, a bunk. Cory lay in the bunk, his eyes closed and the flush of fever upon him, his body turned slightly to favor his left arm. His sleeve had been cut away and his arm was crudely bandaged, but dried blood showed. Ives looked at him in the lamplight and said to Marybelle, "How did you find him?" Oddly, he'd not wondered about that till now.

"His horse came home," Marybelle said. "The sign said it came down out of the north. I tried back-trailing it as far as I could. Rod Benedict had given up the same notion. The hill country is too rocky. But I began riding circles. It seemed to me that if a person were wounded they would try to head for some sort of shelter. This place is the only one up here."

Ives nodded. Cory's breathing was shallow, but his pulse seemed sound enough; pain had pulled his mouth out of shape. Ives removed Marybelle's bandage and looked at the wound; it was in the upper arm, and it didn't look good, and Ives's fear was that the arm might have to come off. He wondered if he should tell the girl this; he had a hunch she would take it without flinching.

He walked to the table and tested its sturdiness. He lifted the lamp to one of the chairs, and said, "Tom, give me a hand. We're going to move him to the table."

They got hold of Cory and lifted him from the bunk to the table top and spread him out, Marybelle helping. Ives said then, "I'm going after the bullet. Build up a fire in the stove. fill everything you can find with water. There's a well out in the yard."

"Yes," she said.

"Find every piece of white cloth you can. Put them in

one of the kettles to boil. Tom, there's a black case tied to my saddle. Fetch it here.''

Feather shuffled away obediently; Marybelle was already doing as she'd been directed. Ives opened his case when it was brought to him; he had chloroform, but he decided not to use it. The vapors of the drug, exposed to the flame of a kerosene lamp, produced an irritating gas. He dumped his instruments into one of the kettles Marybelle had placed upon the stove. The girl was keeping the fire going; she sent Feather to fill a depleted woodbox, and the water was boiled half an hour. Ives spent this time studying the wound and making his calculations. He scrubbed his hands thoroughly, pouring a chemical into the tin wash basin. He was concerned with possible infection; this shack was filthy. Clean, rapid work would minimize Cory's danger.

''There may be other lamps around,'' Ives said shortly. ''Rustle them up.''

Marybelle found two lamps in a cupboard. The wicks trimmed and the chimneys cleaned, the three were placed upon a shelf so that the light fell from above. Ives had Marybelle scour tin plates and put them behind the lamps for reflectors. This done, Ives directed her to string a rope across a corner of the room and hang one of the blankets from the bunk upon it; he would have preferred a white sheet to catch the light and throw it back, but there was no sheet.

These things done, he placed the dishpan with the instruments upon a chair and was ready to fall to work. He looked at Tom Feather and said then, ''Get out front, Tom. Keep an eye peeled, will you? Might be a fellow riding up on a white horse. If he comes, keep him busy out there till I'm finished.''

Feather left the shack, and Marybelle said, ''What's this about a man on a white horse?''

"I invented him," Ives said absently. "I just don't want Tom underfoot when I really go to work."

She said, "He belongs to Hammer. Suppose he heads down there and tells Carradine that Cory's lying helpless here?"

"He won't go," Ives said.

"You've known him for a long time?"

"All my life. He came up from Texas with the colonel, I believe. He's a sort of pensioner. Hammer feeds him and clothes him, but he does as he pleases. He's crazy, of course. Mostly, he's still living in Texas, but he has lucid moments. Don't let him worry you."

"He called you Jim."

"I know," he said and frowned. "It didn't make sense to me, either. But maybe it will. Maybe it will."

He bent to his work; he became oblivious to the girl and the cabin and the night; he sought the elusive lead, turning his head only when he had to reach for an instrument. The lamps were too near, and the blanket threw back their heat as well as their light, and sweat came to blind him, but still he worked. Silence held the cabin; once he looked up to see Marybelle across the table; she was staring fixedly at her brother's arm, but Ives didn't think she was going to faint.

Cory came to partial consciousness; a babble poured from his writhing lips. They always talked. Some of them cursed and some of them prayed; and Ives had made his judgment as to which Cory would do, and there lay the surprise. The words were formless and all tangled, but the idiom of the ancient Book was in them. Ives remembered Elisha Lund then and understood; these were the things Cory had learned at his father's knee and they mixed into his torment now and sustained him.

Once Cory opened his eyes, and Ives wished that he'd used the chloroform. Cory tried to raise himself, and Ives said sharply, "Lie still!" Cory sank back upon the table; his eyes closed, and his face was a dead man's face.

A moment later Ives said, "The basin." Marybelle extended the empty wash basin and something rattled in it, and Ives said, "There's the slug. Forty-five, I'd guess."

Marybelle said, "And every man along the Sombra packs one."

He nodded and busied himself at the bandaging. Marybelle had found very little to qualify for bandages, but the cloths had been boiled and left to dry, and Ives did the best he could. When he was finished, he stepped back, the sweat coming down and blinding him, and he sluiced it away with his sleeve.

Cory opened his eyes and looked hard at him and said, "So it's you!"

Ives said, "Lie back and sleep, if you can. You'll be all right now."

Cory muttered something but did as he was told. His breathing had grown stronger, he fell into a natural sleep, but there was a little of the fever left in it. Ives took his pulse, finding it unchanged. He said, "Later we'll move him back to the bunk, if we can." He took a step and found that he staggered. "I'm done in."

He yanked the blanket down from the line and walked to the door and stepped outside and sat upon the sill. It was always this way afterward, this feeling triumphant and defeated all in one. Tom Feather shaped up in the darkness and squatted on his heels not far away. Ives smiled and said, "That jigger show up?"

Feather said nothing, and in Ives was the thought that now was the time to do another kind of digging—now was the chance that had been denied him at Hammer yesterday and at this cabin earlier tonight. He thought: *He knows—he knows—* but he was empty with the feeling that the things Tom Feather knew might be as tangled and aimless as the words that had fallen from Cory's delirious lips. Yet the feeling was also strong in him that he stood now before a closed door that might be opened by his touch, and in a last moment of hesitancy he wondered if he wanted that door opened.

Then he said softly, "Tom, speak up. It's me—Jim. You remember Jim?"

Feather held his silence a moment longer, and then he said in a voice of bewilderment, "You're a sawbones. I looked in the window and watched you. You ain't Jim. Jim was no sawbones. What in tarnation was it made me think you was Jim?"

Ives said desperately, "Keep talking! Tell me all about Jim!"

Feather said, "I'm all mixed up again. I should have knowed when you sent me for the black case. A sawbones!" He came to a stand and shambled off, and Ives let him go. There was no way of bringing Tom Feather back; the distance was more than the width of a stump-strewn clearing—the distance was infinite.

Marybelle came to the door and stepped out. She seated herself beside Ives and leaned her shoulder against his, and suddenly he knew that this night had taken as much toll of her as it had of him. He was struggling with his own disappointment, but there was room for sympathy in him. He put his arm around her shoulder and drew her close and let her weight lie against him.

7

Saddle and Ride

THEY SAT IN SILENCE FOR A LONG TIME, THE NIGHT around them, but in Marybelle's nearness was as much eloquence as Ives needed. Once, as a boy, he had built a raft and poled it along the bank of the Sombra, and it had been easy going and he was master of the raft. But sometimes he became absorbed in a blue jay's chatter or a cloud formation or a lift of dust on a distant butte, and at such times the raft edged out into the current, and he felt the insidious grip of the river and knew he was being pulled beyond his depth. He had the same sensation now. The girl was here, seemingly exerting no influence upon him, seemingly as quiet as the pools along the Sombra; but he could feel the current. Still, he kept his arm around her.

She said, "I'm tired."

He was reflecting upon how close they had grown in such a short time. He recalled their first meeting. Had they been meant to short-cut to each other, to arrive directly at some destination without tortuous windings? Yet she did not interest him, really, not as Marybelle Lund, a woman and desirable. He was thinking that she belonged to one faction and he to another: he had pitted himself against Colonel Carradine that afternoon, yet his lot was irrevocably cast with the colonel, and he had a wounded scalp for proof of it. But perhaps he and this girl wanted the same thing, peace along the Sombra, and perhaps they were already allies in that cause.

He said, "Marybelle?"

"Yes?" she said sleepily.

"What is it you want out of life?"

She needed no pause for reflection. "The same as any woman. Security."

He said, "A home and a husband? Children? Ground to plow with no need to have a rifle handy?"

She said, "One way or another, a man would probably always need his rifle. I can't change that. So I won't worry about it."

He turned this over in his mind. "Then it doesn't really matter to you whether Carradine imports gunmen?"

"It matters, yes. But what can I do about it? I was only a child when I learned that I couldn't shape people to my way. I gave that up long ago. Now I spend most of my time thinking of myself."

He said, "That's selfish!"

"No, it's just blunt," she said. The sleepiness was gone from her voice. "Men fool themselves into the notion that they think in a larger sense than women. Actually, men are after the same thing—security. But they reason that they have to gain security by crowding their neighbors. A woman is more direct. She narrows her need down to essentials. Is that so wicked?"

He said, "But you fetched me up here tonight for Cory's sake. And for something bigger, I hoped. Cory, dead, could have set the nesters on the warpath."

"Cory's my brother," she said. "He's quite a bit of a fool, but he's my brother. That's what I was thinking about.

If his staying alive keeps the homesteaders from oiling their guns, so much the better. Does that answer you?''

He said slowly, ''I'm trying to put all the pieces together and make some sense out of them.''

She laughed. ''You're trying to see me as a reflection of yourself. That's what any man does when he meets a woman who interests him. And you're interested.''

''I'll not deny it,'' he said. ''But I want to believe that hardness of yours is only a pretense.''

''I'm shameless, Doc,'' she said. ''You already know that. You might as well know that I've set my cap for you.''

He had to smile. He remembered the potatoes he'd taken for payment for his services in Oregon. He said, ''I'm a poor bet—a mighty poor bet. Do you know how much security you'd get out of a saddlebag sawbones?''

''All I'd need, if the sawbones were you, Doc. You see, it's more than a matter of four walls and food on the table and a new dress to wear to a dance. You'd give me the real security that all of us are after—the security of knowing I was owned and therefore would be protected because I'd be the most priceless of all properties. Yes, Doc, I'll have security when I have you.''

''And it will never matter what the rest of the world is doing? Even when the flames lick at our own doorstep?''

''You'll do the worrying about that, and I'll help you whenever I can. That's the way it'll be. No, I'm not completely heartless. I'm just practical. That should make a fine balance between us.''

He said, ''You're amazing! Amazing!''

She began to speak again, her voice suddenly far away and dreamy; she spoke of Minnesota and she spoke of the Dakotas. He saw a God-fearing father and a work-worn mother and a brother with wildness in him; he saw desolate quarter sections and men pitting themselves against the adamant earth, and tattered wagons silhouetted against a setting sun, and a people trying it farther west. Uncarpeted floors were in her talk, and skimpy meals and tilted outhouses and hair ribbons at Christmas time and mailorder catalogs bulging with things that were always beyond reach. Desolation and emptiness—these things were painted for him; and he remembered his own boyhood and Hammer's house, and it became a palace by comparison.

When she had finished, the ghost of weeping was in her voice. She said then, "Don't think me made of iron. If my father could sink his roots here and keep them planted, that would make me happy. Any man should own at least as much earth as he needs to be buried in. Yes, I'd like peace along the Sombra. But I've seen all this before; I've sat in a wagon and had my mother tell me not to look back because if I had, I would have seen our shack in flames. I know that may happen again. Do you wonder that I'm looking for a different life?"

He shook his head. "I wonder if you'll find it. Or is the defeat something inside you, something you'll never be able to run away from?"

She said, "I've wondered that, too. I'm not always sure of myself."

Both stood up. In the light that fell from the open doorway, he looked at her intently; he raised his hands and put them on her shoulders, his eyes grave, his eyes kindly. "Good luck, little girl," he said.

Her smile turned roguish. "Who'll need the luck, Doc? Remember, I've got my cap set for you."

Cory's voice reached them; it was an incoherent mumble, but it touched Ives and awoke the medico in him. He stepped inside the shack. Cory was trying to turn on his side; his bandaged arm prevented him.

Ives said, "He should be put back in the bunk." He

stepped to the door and cupped his hands to his mouth and called, "Tom! Tom Feather!" He listened then; the wind murmured in the pine tops, somewhere a distant creek gurgled, an owl slid by on silent wings, hunting. Ives turned back into the shack.

"He's gone," he said. He walked to the table and carefully got one arm under Cory's shoulders, the other under the boy's knees. He lifted Cory and staggered to the bunk with him, being very careful about that arm.

Marybelle said, "You're stronger than you look."

Cory's eyes opened. Ives said, "How are you feeling?"

Cory said, "Fagged out."

Ives said, "If you feel up to it, I'd like to know who shot you."

Cory tried shaking his head. "It was last night, I guess. What day is this?"

"Tuesday. Maybe Wednesday now."

"The day I met you in town. I rode out. Took a swing up toward the hills. Just riding. Somebody shot me from cover. I fell—off horse. Crawled and crawled. I knew there was a shack up here."

"You didn't see the bushwhacker?"

"Never—saw—him."

"Sleep, now," Ives urged. "That's what you need. Sleep." He took Cory's pulse again, automatically.

Marybelle said, "We ought to get him out of here."

Ives shook his head. "He can't be moved. Not for a while. He might have lost that arm. I should have got here sooner." He began a prowling of the shack that seemed aimless but was actually a thorough searching of all cupboards. He said then, "We'll have to have food up here. And I want clean white cloth so the wound can be redressed. The colonel doesn't keep this place stocked at this season."

He paused, lost in reflection. Then he said, "I'll ride to Hammer.I think I can make it there before dawn."

She said, "You could stay with Cory. I could ride to the settlement."

"As the crow flies, it's closer to Hammer. That means that I'll be the one who goes. He won't need me, not until he's slept himself out. You're not afraid of staying here alone?"

"I'm not afraid," she said. "I just don't want Hammer to know he's here. That's why I was worried about that crazy old fellow, Feather. If Carradine could chop down Cory, he'd have taken the fighting leader from the homesteaders. Sure, my father is really the leader, but Cory will be up front if they ride to war."

Ives said, "If it will make you feel better, Hammer won't know. But I've still got to go after those things."

She said, "You know best."

He went to the door, and again he cupped his hands to his mouth and called Tom Feather. The night had stolen Tom Feather; the night had whisked him away.

Ives walked to his horse; Marybelle walked with him. Feather had unsaddled both mounts and dumped the gear upon a bench before the shack; Ives got one of the saddles and slapped it up the back of the horse he'd ridden from Tamerlane. He climbed into the saddle and said absently, "When this gets settled, I'll have a look in at that Jensen place," and he realized then that the pacing nester and Marybelle's report of a sick child had been gnawing at the fringes of his consciousness all night.

Marybelle said, "When you start that, you'll have your hands full. There are several sick children in the settlement."

"What seems to ail them?"

She shook her head. "Who knows? We've had no doctor here. It's something the children have caught from each other, because they've all acted the same. Headaches and backaches, and they won't eat. Stomach pains."

"I'll look into that," he said and clucked the horse to motion.

He was too tired for real thinking, but part of his mind was alert, and that part of it probed for the truth. Not until the shack was lost to his view did the truth hit him, and it came so startlingly that he jerked hard at the reins, bringing the horse to a halt. He said aloud, "Typhoid! My God, typhoid fever!" And dread was in him.

For a moment he was all doctor, and the need of the nesters overwhelmed him; and then he jogged the horse again, still heading for Hammer. Cory Lund was a patient, too; there had to be a first thing first. Cory's sickness might become an entire range's sickness, more devastating even than a typhoid epidemic. He told himself he was jumping at shadows, but fear still nagged at him. He tried putting it from his mind; he tried thinking of other things; he considered the disjointed tale Cory had told of how he'd come to stop a bullet. Ives's thought was that both of them had met with a bushwhacker on the same day. He wondered then if Brule could have been behind the gun that had pitched Cory out of his saddle, but he wasn't sure enough of the factors of time and space to know whether this was possible.

The trail he followed looped ever downward, the timber thinning out but the darkness still holding though the dawn was not far away. He kept in the general direction of Hammer, riding by instinct; out of the hills, he felt the immensity of space again, and sometimes he was sure he was lost. He kept straining his eyes for the first twinkle of lamplight; surely in that great ranch at least one lamp would be showing. He kept straining his ears for the bark of a dog. He came upon bedded cattle; he skirted these. Always he rode warily, remembering that a gun that had spoken twice could speak still a third time.

Then he was upon Hammer; in the gloom the buildings

didn't shape up until he was almost in the yard, and it was the dog that gave him his inkling, just as he'd expected. The dog circled around him, leaping and barking and making the horse fiddle-footed; and Ives came down from the saddle and soothed the dog and groped toward the house. It lay dark.

The silence here was far too heavy; the silence clamored in the yard. He couldn't have put a name to the feeling that came over him then; he only knew that something was almighty wrong with Hammer, and he hurried to the door, though in his haste there was a strange reluctance.

8

Thunder over Tamerlane

MARCO STOLL, AFTER HIS TALK WITH BRIAN IVES through the window of the Tamerlane jail, had melted into the shadows, and thereafter he appeared on the street's planking, an unobtrusive figure in spite of his bulk, a man seemingly indolent and without any real business abroad. He might have been taking the air. He waddled the length of the street, speaking to many people in passing but saying no more than a brief, "Good evening." There was no time for small talk among the gathered men; Stoll could tell that. They stood in twos and threes and fours, talking low-voiced, talking with an edge of temper to their voices, and Stoll noticed that mostly they stood in shadows. That was significant, and the significance was not lost upon him. Light is for levity and camaraderie and careless talk. Tamerlane's people had something on their minds tonight.

The street was a pattern of light and dark; the saloons and such business establishments as were still open threw lamplight out upon the planking and the dust beyond; between these intermittent oases the darkness lay. Stoll completed his round and turned in at his drugstore, opening the door with a key he carried. The place was dark, the pimply clerk long gone home. Stoll debated a moment, then left the door unlocked, but he lighted no lamp. He crossed to the stairs and wheezed up them and moved familiarly within his own quarters, not once imperiling any piece of furniture in the crowded room.

His black felt hat he placed carefully on an antler hat-rack; and, because the evening was warm, he pulled himself out of his coat and hung this upon the rack, too. Then he eased into his chair by the window. The window had been left open; from here he had seen Ives ride in earlier as Rod Benedict's prisoner. From here Stoll had seen Tamerlane across the years. He sat now and let time pile up; he sat with his eyes on the street, his full-moon face benevolent and placid. He sat in the darkness and waited.

From below, those muted voices rose to him; sometimes he even caught a coherent word when anger put a sharp vehemence to it, but he made no real effort to hear the words. The tone of the voices told him all he needed to know—the tone and the remembrance that the men who spoke wore denim. He watched the hitchrails of such saloons as were within his range of vision. Most of the hitchrails were empty. It was too early in the evening for the cattlemen to have come for their drinking, and they came less often these days, anyway. Tamerlane, it was said, was forbidden to Hammer's crew, but there were ranches on the far side of the Sombra. He thought about this. Cattlemen clung to their kind, and Brian Ives, he supposed, was their kind. But here was an imponderable without any real answer.

Rod Benedict came within his range of vision, the sheriff's long arms and legs swinging; Stoll saw the black and white of the calfskin vest, and spilled lamplight caught the ball-pointed star and reflected from it. Benedict paused in the shadows and spoke to one of the gathered groups; his voice reached Stoll; the voice held a feigned carelessness, the voice might have been pleading in its own way. Stoll smiled, remembering that Benedict was half and half, part cowman, part sodbuster; and he wondered how many farmers were remembering that tonight.

He reached and fingered one of the chessmen, lifting it in his hand, seeming to weigh it, then placing it back upon the board. He was not conscious of what he had done.

Benedict had swung on down the street, his voice calling back a good night to the group he'd just left. Benedict was a man trying to dam a tide of disaster with cheerful talk. Stoll smiled again, but the smile faded and became a frown. Benedict would talk only while there was time for talking; after that Benedict would act and his actions would be in his own fashion. There was an old saying—you could take a boy out of Texas, but you couldn't take Texas out of the boy.

Elisha Lund appeared on the porch of the mercantile store, which was still open. The homesteader leader stood there, a gaunt, grim statue of a man who looked upon the town broodingly. Lund had come by a conviction in Tamerlane's jail; Stoll, out in the shadows, waiting his chance to speak to Ives, had heard that conviction voiced. Lund was also an imponderable; Lund had a dead son to remember tonight. But Lund would cling to a principle. The question was how much weight there was to Lund, and it was Stoll's thought that no one man could stem the fury, not even Elisha Lund.

Lund came down from the porch finally and moved slowly along the street; the shadows caught him and dissolved him to nothingness and then he materialized again, farther along. He, too, stopped to speak to a gathered group. His huge hands moved emphatically; his deep voice carried to Stoll, but the words were lost in distance.

Stoll heard the hoofbeats then; they were far away and

faint, but they were hoofbeats, and he stiffened and even leaned from the window, but suddenly he knew that he was hearing the hoofbeats of only one horse, and the slackness came into him; he settled back in his chair, his rubbery lips drawn down in disappointment. The lone horseman appeared in Tamerlane's street; he was a gaunt, overall-clad man riding bareback upon a gaunt farm horse. He drew to a halt before the drugstore, fell from the horse, hastily wrapped a tie rope around the hitchrail and lurched across the sidewalk. He shook the drugstore door, and, finding it open, stumbled inside.

His voice reached through the building frantically, "Stoll! Mr. Stoll! You here?"

Stoll sighed, coming out of the chair and waddling across the room; and from the top of the stairs he shouted, "Drugstore's closed for the night."

"I got to have medicine!" the man below insisted.

Stoll sighed again; he wanted to be rid of this man and he did a hasty weighing of factors and his conclusion was that he'd be sooner rid of the fellow by serving him. Stoll said, "Just a minute, I'll be down."

In the drugstore, he found the man restlessly pacing; Stoll knew this man; his name was Beamis, and he was one of the settlers on the upper Sombra. Stoll put on his professional voice, and said, "What's the trouble, Beamis?"

"My little girl. She's sick. She's been getting worse. I just had to come to town."

"What ails her?"

"She ain't been eating right. And she's had headaches and backaches and says her belly hurts her. Jensen's little boy has been acting the same way. And Gunderson's. It's enough to drive a man crazy!"

Stoll waddled behind his prescription counter and got a wall lamp burning; the light threw a long shadow behind

Beamis; the light made Beamis chalky and sick-looking, and his shadow paced with him and filled the room with weird movement.

Stoll said soothingly, "We'll fix her up."

Beamis said, "What do you suppose is the matter?"

"Summer complaint," Stoll judged. "Kids all get it this time of year."

He reached to a shelf and took down a battered, brown copy of *Griffith's Universal Formulary* as revised by Thomas; this edition bore the date 1859 and had belonged to many druggists and had served Stoll a long time. He opened to the table of contents, fumbled in his vest pocket for his glasses, adjusted them on his nose and ran a fat finger to the notation *Index of Diseases and Their Remedies.* He turned the pages to this section and ran his finger down the alphabetized list of diseases until he came to *Stomach, Affections of.* He began reading aloud, "Oxide of silver, 126, Sub-nitrate of bismuth, 148—"

He took off his glasses and laid them on the book to hold it open at the place and went about mixing the prescription. When it was finished and handed to Beamis, the farmer said, "I can't pay you for this just now."

Stoll waved a fat hand. "I'll put it on the books."

"I'm obliged," Beamis said with great sincerity. "Oh, another thing. My little girl's getting some red spots on her belly."

Stoll was extinguishing the lamp; he paused in this act, stiff with a new knowledge; he paused, but only for a second, his need to get rid of this man strong in him, and then his breath engulfed the flame, and in the darkness he said, "Probably nothing to worry about. If that medicine doesn't do her any good, come back and I'll give you something different."

Beamis said bitterly, "The word's around that there's a doctor here now. A doctor who belongs to Hammer."

Stoll said, "You might as well forget about him."

He saw Beamis to the door; he watched the man haul himself onto his horse and head back out of town at a high lope, and Stoll debated then as to whether to lock the door. He wanted it open, and he decided that the odds were against another interruption tonight; and he closed the door, climbed the stairs again and found his way to his chair.

Nothing had changed. Those groups were still gathered on the street; and after Stoll had waited a while, Rod Benedict passed below, still cheerful, having time for each group, still playing out his patient game of waiting. Lund appeared, too; he strode along, coming into Stoll's range of vision and passing beyond it; and Stoll weighed Lund's continued presence in town and found it significant. Lund was no night owl; Lund, ordinarily, would have long since gone home. Lund was waiting, too.

And then the thunder of hoofs came again.

This time there was no mistaking that many riders were in the saddle, and they were coming at a high lope, they were coming out of the north. And now whatever there was of tension in Stoll left him, and he was a man satisfied. This was something like the mixing of a prescription; you put in this ingredient with that ingredient and you added still another, and the results were preordained. Tonight he had made his secret bet with himself that things would come about as they had, and he had won.

The riders were spilling into the street, and they came as Texas men had always come, at a high lope and with the guns banging. They came as the trail drovers of another day had come to Sedalia and Abilene and Dodge City and all the trail towns, crowding their horses and loosing their thunder; and the false fronts of Tamerlane caught the sounds and sent them beating back in growing waves, and horsemen were everywhere, and their rallying cry went up, "Hammer! Hammer!"

They spread out, encompassing the street, and the thunder of guns rolled over Tamerlane, but there was no real danger. Most of the guns were blasting at the sky, but the fury of them was intimidating; men were rushing to cover, those same men who had stood in groups through the evening and made their sullen talk. One denim-clad man making a move for a gun, one farmer showing fight might have changed all this, but there was no one farmer to take the lead. Elisha Lund might have done it. But Lund had gained a conviction tonight.

Colonel Carradine was in the center of the chaos Hammer wrought. He sat a rearing, pitching saddle almost directly below the drugstore; light fell upon him, and his white hair was flying, and his goatee bristled a great defiance. In the saddle he was Dixie's ill-fated flag still flying; he was power and invincibility, and the people of Tamerlane quailed before him. His voice carried shouted orders; his guns glittered in his hand, and he sat lean and straight and black-clad, a part of his horse.

Someone came thundering up the street from the direction of the jail house; someone who cried, "He's not there, Colonel. Door's wide open and the place is empty!"

"Look in the sheriff's house then," Carradine shouted. "He must be here in town."

In the street was constant movement and constant sound, hoofs roiling the dust, guns blazing, and only the colonel staying in the one spot. Glass tinkled; a random shot had taken out a window. A man's boots beat frantically along the boardwalk; this man stumbled and fell and lay sobbing with fear. Hammer had treed Tamerlane. All this seemed endless; all this was brief and hurried and noisy and soon over. A man came slithering to a stop near the colonel, his horse rearing. "Nobody at the sheriff's but his mother," the man bawled.

"Then we'll look elsewhere," Carradine cried.

And still no man made a move against Hammer. Hammer held the street, and the darkness was filled with cowering figures, and a great sickness was in Marco Stoll.

Below him was the colonel, and Stoll's fingers reached out and fastened upon the shotgun which leaned near the window, and he raised the shotgun and put it down again; there was that much wisdom to stay his anger. A shotgun charge would be the same as his signature. He got out of the chair quickly and crossed to the antler rack. From it hung a belt with holster and gun; he lifted the gun from leather and with this Colt's forty-five in his hand, went back to the window. Hammer's men were rallying around the colonel; soon they would be bunched and charging out of town. But there was this moment.

Stoll raised the gun and tilted its barrel downward and looked along the barrel; the colonel was square in the sights.

In this crowded moment there was all the time a man needed for remembering; Stoll could look forward and backward at the same time, and the things that were behind needed no recalling, they had stayed too poignantly alive. But ahead—

The colonel stiff in a coffin, a coroner's jury, mostly in denim, listening stolidly. Testimony of a thunderous night and many men with hate in them, some with guns within reach. One of Hammer's crew—possibly the foreman—kneading his sombrero in his hands and saying, "Enemies? Sure, the colonel had lots of enemies. Stoll? Well, Stoll was never allowed on Hammer, but none of us rightly knew what the trouble was about. Unless it might be old Tom Feather."

That was the only risk, that someone might figure out

that the bullet had been fired from above and for a while the finger of suspicion might be pointed. Yet it was only the shadow of a risk, and thus this was Stoll's moment, and the colonel was there in his sights.

And then Stoll lowered the gun unfired and let it slip from his fingers and clatter to the floor, and a torrent of emotion was shaking him, threaded by only one coherent thought: *Not yet! Not yet!*

The colonel wheeled his horse and spurred it along the street, still brandishing his gun; his crew fell in behind him, and they left Tamerlane as they had come, crowding their horses, filling the air with thunder.

Stoll watched them go. He heard men hurrying from the cover of doorways and the slots between buildings, but he was blind to what there was to see, and deaf to what there was to hear.

For a long time he merely sat, and finally the trembling went out of him, and he reached to the chessboard and fingered the pieces and was satisfied with himself. He had had his temptation; he had overridden it, and there lay the great satisfaction—he had not sold himself short.

After a while he heard the door below open and close again; he heard boots move across the drugstore floor and the stairs creak. The man who framed himself in the doorway to Stoll's living-quarters was square-cut and had a brutish hunch to his shoulders and he favored one leg, putting his weight on the other.

Stoll said, "Nobody saw you come in?"

Brule shrugged. "I don't think so." He waited a moment. "A hot time in the old town tonight."

Stoll said, "But their bird had flown its cage. Now why was that?"

Brule said, "I wouldn't know. The colonel certainly kicked over a hornet's nest. A dozen men could have got him fair and square. Ain't there any guts in these sodbusters?''

Stoll said, ''I'm beginning to wonder.'' He stirred himself in the chair. ''I'll go down and lock the front door. I don't want some fool walking in here and finding you.''

Brule grinned. ''I might be after medicine for a snake bite.''

''Yes,'' Stoll said. ''You might.'' He lost himself in reflection for a moment. ''If you were Brian Ives, and you decided to walk out of jail, where would you head?''

Brule gave this his careful consideration. ''The Sombra Hills,'' he said then.

9

The Bushwhacker

WHEN BRIAN IVES, GROPING IN THE DARKNESS BEFORE dawn, found his way across the gallery of Hammer's ranch house to the door, he knocked upon it. This was the only home he'd ever known, yet he knocked upon the door. The dog had accepted him; the dog came with him to the gallery, nuzzling at his hand and whining softly. He found a strange comfort in that. But the silence still held, the silence still clamored, and the first dread remained with him. He knocked again, then listened intently. Someone moved in the depth of the house. He heard the bar lifted; the door opened, and Tana stood there.

He said, "It's me—Brian."

She wore a flowered dressing-gown over her nightgown. In her right hand was a Colt's forty-five; it looked big and ponderous and all out of proportion. She looked at him, not saying anything; and then the gun sagged until it was pointed at her feet, and she teetered, and his fear was that she was going to faint.

She said, "Come in. Oh, come in!"

He moved into the house and closed the door after him

and dropped the bar back into place. He could sense that she was moving in the darkness; he heard a match scrape and a lamp threw its circle of light. They were in the house's biggest room; it was a room of books and rawhide-bottomed chairs, centered by a table littered with magazines. Some of these were stockmen's journals; a few copies of *Godey's Lady's Book* were lying in view. Tana placed the gun on the table; her black hair, braided for the night, hung in two braids down her back. She seated herself upon a divan which stood against one wall.

She said, "You got out of jail?"

He said quickly, "Cory Lund's alive. He got a slug in his arm. He managed to make it to Feather's shack. His sister found him there. She came to town for me. Benedict was careless with the key, and there was no trouble. I dug the slug out of Cory."

She rocked back and forth. "Knowing that might have made all the difference," she said hopelessly. "A few hours ago."

"The colonel's gone?" He waved an arm aimlessly, taking in the entire house.

"Everyone's gone. To Tamerlane. To snatch you out of jail."

He remembered the guns then; he remembered wanting to turn back to Tamerlane and Marybelle urging him to go on to the hills. He began pacing the room. "The colonel will have blown the lid right off!" he said.

"He was a madman after Rod rode away with you in the afternoon," Tana said. "For a long, long time, he just sat staring. Then he took to pacing like a caged tiger. He didn't touch his supper. Afterward he called the crew to the gallery and gave them orders. They saddled up and left. That was hours ago."

Ives measured time and distance in his mind and said, "They found me missing, of course. Then why aren't they back?" But he knew why they weren't back; he knew where Carradine would have carried his search. He said, his voice empty, "The colonel must have supposed I was whisked out of town. If he's gone to the nester settlement to search every shack, we might as well figure that the war's on."

Tana said, "Yes, yes—"

Ives made a fist and beat it against his left palm. He said, "That isn't at all the way you hoped it would be, is it? You sent for me to save him from his own folly; but because I came here, the lid blew off."

"That wasn't your fault," she said. "I heard what you said to him on the gallery this afternoon. It was everything that could have been said. Yes, I hoped that you'd be able to show him that he was heading to his own destruction. I'd tried and failed. Lately, he's treated me the way he used to treat you—with a cold politeness. Each day we've grown further apart. So in desperation I wrote to you."

He said, "What did you think I could do, really?"

She said, "Who else could I have turned to?"

He'd never thought about that before; there were many things he'd never thought about. He looked at Tana, seeing a woman. The two years' difference in their ages counted no longer; once those years had been a great gap. The pair of them had grown up on this ranch together, but she'd never been a younger sister to him. She had been a grave, aloof girl who had shown him little kindnesses in her own quiet fashion, and those had been the bright spots of the buried years. Quite often she'd been gone from the ranch—to schools in the East. He'd always been glad to see her return, but he'd never so much as touched her hand.

Now he looked at her and knew their real kinship; she had grown up under the shadow of the colonel, too. And she had remembered a certain Brian Ives and turned to him in her desperate hour. He came to the divan and sat down beside her and took her hand in his and said, "Let's hope everything isn't lost yet."

She turned and looked at him and she was trembling and then suddenly she slid against him, not as though this were a conscious move but as though strength had left her. Their shoulders touched; he put his arms around her and drew her close; beneath the thin gown her breasts thrust hard against him; and, without meaning to, he kissed her. Her mouth clung to his, and he knew her then for the first time; he knew that serenity had been her only armor and it was stripped from her now, and she was all woman with a woman's hunger and a woman's need. The kiss was her surrender, and it was complete, and they were alone in this great house; and the awareness of this throbbed in Ives's temples.

Then she was pushing him away from her, her hands beating at his chest, her breath coming in sobs; and he drew back from her and stood up. Shame came upon him, and he said, "I'm sorry. I know how it is. There's Benedict."

"Rod?" she said, startled.

"He's in love with you."

She said, "I wasn't thinking of him. I was thinking of us. We must never let this happen again."

He said, "I think we've both been too damn lonely for too damn long."

"It was only half your fault, Brian. Forgive me. We've both got to remember that it just couldn't be."

Only then did he sense the real truth, and it was half glimpsed; it was like seeing a vista of prairie lighted up by a sudden lightning flash, then plunged into darkness again. He stepped closer to her; he stood towering over her; looking down, he could see the shadowy V of her breasts, but he was unmoved. He said, "Two things brought me home, and your sending for me was one of them. The other was something that I thought didn't really matter, but it always has. You know, don't you?"

"Know what, Brian?"

"Who I am. Who my folks were."

She bowed her head; she kept it bowed and thus there was no meeting of their eyes. She said nothing.

"Tom Feather knows, too," he insisted. "Tom might tell me, but he's addled and the years are all mixed up for him. But you could tell me. You know, don't you?"

She nodded.

He stood waiting; somewhere in the house a clock ticked; he remembered the clock, a banjo clock on the wall of the colonel's bedroom. It had measured out many years.

"When you left," she said, "when you went to Wyoming and read medicine, I cried."

"You cried for me?" He was astounded.

"I cried," she said, "and the colonel took me to his study and told me all of it. That was ten years ago."

He remembered the lowing of cattle beneath a darkling sky; he remembered his recurring fear forever tied to that sound; and he remembered, too, the teacher and her jingle: "As I was going to St. Ives—" He tried to still the trembling within him. He said, "I'm waiting, Tana."

Her voice was so low he could scarcely hear it. She said, "Will you believe it's better that you don't know? Will you believe that the only reason I can't tell you is because you mean a very great deal to me?"

He thought of Tom Feather. "The roots of this thing were in Texas," he guessed.

"Yes," she said.

He said, "Is that all you can tell me?"

She said, "I'll have to ask you for faith."

He stood looking down upon her for a long moment, a tumult of emotions in him, and then he reached for her.

He got his hands under her arms; he could feel the lift of her breasts against the heels of his hands. He brought her to her feet, and he raised her chin with the knuckle of his right index finger and kissed her again, not putting his arms around her. It was a gentle kiss that erased the first one. He stepped back from her.

"I need some things," he said briskly. "Food. Some cloth for bandages. A couple of clean sheets will do. I can tear them to size."

"I'll get them for you, Brian."

"Young Lund may have to stay where he is for a few days. There's nothing much up at the shack."

She walked from the room; he crossed to a window and shot up the blind; the east was showing its first faint light. He could hear her moving about in a distant part of the house. He waited; she came back tugging a gunny sack that bulged with canned goods.

"I put the sheets inside the sack," she said.

He took the sack from her and walked toward the door. "I've got to get back at once. If you want, you can make a ride for me today. Go to Tamerlane and find your Rod Benedict. Tell him about Cory Lund; tell him everything. If the nesters aren't up in arms yet, maybe that will stop them. Our only chance is that the colonel hasn't yet bought a full-sized war."

She said, "I'll do that, Brian."

There was an aliveness to her; he had done that much by this brief visit. He smiled at her, knowing then how dear she was to him, feeling a closeness he had never known before. He said, "We'll make out, you and I."

She said, "Good luck, Brian."

"I'll be back at Hammer as soon as my patient is able to sit a saddle and get to his own home."

She lifted the bar for him and closed the door behind him. Faint gray light washed the yard now, and the silent ranch had lost its dread. He fastened the sack to the saddle and stepped up and turned his face to the north. He rode along with the light growing stronger and the grass glistening with dew and the meadow larks caroling the dawn. He rode with a deep inner satisfaction that was at first nameless until he traced it to its roots, and its roots were Tana. He had known no family, not really, and he had found a sister. That was good. Yet the memory of that first kiss was still with him, and his thought was that it would take some living to bury that memory.

He was able to make better time than on his trip down from the hills, but soon he was climbing and he had to go easy on the horse. Stunted trees studded the buttes, and from a high lift of ground he could look back toward Hammer and see smoke lifting from the ranch house. That would be Tana preparing breakfast before the ride to town. He looked to where the willows marched along Sombra River; he thought of the colonel and frowned, wondering if Tana's ride might be in vain.

Then the airlash of the bullet came, and the echoing bark of the gun.

He fell out of the saddle; that was pure instinct. Hitting the ground, he rolled, came up on his hands and knees and scuttled crab-fashion for a nest of rocks near by. He got into these rocks; they were slippery with dew and none of them was high enough, and he had a naked feeling. He lifted his eyes and peered. Yonder, within six-shooter range, was a clump of gnarled cedars, and from that clump the shot had come.

He expected a second shot, and he wished mightily for his gun. He was going to have to get it out of his carpetbag and keep it handy on this range, but the carpetbag was at Feather's place. He looked toward his horse. As he'd dropped from the saddle, he'd flung the reins out and they had fallen to the ground, anchoring the horse. That mount was range-trained, however Marybelle had come by it. He was glad of that. But he couldn't lie here waiting for the hidden bushwhacker to show himself, to come closer for the *coup de grace*. He'd have to risk a run for the horse and a hard gallop afterward; therein lay his only chance.

He came to a sudden stand and headed for the horse and flung himself into the saddle; he snatched up the reins and wheeled the horse about, expecting the bark of a gun. Then he saw movement over yonder by the cedars; a man spurred from that ambush, riding away, a man bent low over his saddle and quirting his horse. He was visible for a moment but there was no identifying him, not in the early light. The bushwhacker topped a rise and was briefly skylined and then dropped from sight.

Ives watched him go, a great wonderment in him, and then he understood. The bushwhacker had supposed that he, Ives, carried a gun, and the bushwhacker had thought that Ives's rush to the horse signaled an attack. Slowly Ives rode toward the cedar thicket, and in the midst of it he came down from his saddle and looked around. There was sign that a man had stood waiting and that nervousness had had a hold on this man, and he had eased his tension by walking to and fro. And, walking, the man had favored one leg; the sign was mighty plain.

Ives said softly, "Brule."

His thought was: *Twice, now!*

He guessed that Brule had sighted him across the distance and waited here for his quarry to come within six-shooter range. He stood listening; far away he heard the ring of shod hoofs upon rock; the sound diminished and was lost. He climbed into the saddle again and rode onward; soon he was on another promontory that gave him command of a sweep of country. He could see all of Sombra Range, the winding river, the buildings of Hammer, the nester settlement, and, far to the south, the hazy outlines of Tamerlane. He thought he made out a minute speck in the distance, a rider spurring to the southwest. He couldn't be sure.

And so he sat looking upon the Sombra, and the name and its meaning rang in his mind; and he laughed, for there was a shadow on the Sombra, a shadow on the shadow, and he knew now that it was made of more than Colonel Carradine's folly and Elisha Lund's obstinacy and the inevitable sparks that came from one faction pitted against another. He knew that someone was deliberately laying a shadow across this range, and that was why Cory Lund had stopped a bullet and Brian Ives had stopped a bullet and had almost stopped another this morning.

They didn't count, he and Cory; they were puppets on strings, and some unseen hand was manipulating them. No, they were pawns in a game—that analogy suited him better—they were chessmen moved to bring about some far-reaching effect that was beyond guessing.

Oddly then he remembered Marco Stoll's chessboard, and only then was his first suspicion born; but it was a ridiculous suspicion and he banished it as such, exiling the notion to a far corner of his mind. He faced north again, toward Tom Feather's shack, remembering the food he carried, remembering that there would be no breakfast for Marybelle until he arrived.

10

Hostage of Hammer

IVES CAME TOWARD FEATHER'S SHACK CAUTIOUSLY; HE'D learned a few things about caution lately. Once he'd done his riding without fear; he remembered Oregon and how a doctor had been safe there. The only trouble had been the dogs; the dogs hadn't always understood; a stranger was a stranger to them. But with men it had been different. There wasn't a farmer who wouldn't leave his plow to help get a doctor's buggy out of the mud. There wasn't a cowboy who'd refuse to ride fifty miles for medicine if the doctor found he'd forgot to fetch a certain kind along. He had moved across the land with an armor about him, and that armor was the respect of men. But this was the Sombra.

He dismounted before the shack was in view and led his horse through the thickets, approaching the shack so that he didn't have to cross the clearing. When he came around a corner of the building, Marybelle appeared at the door. She looked frightened; he judged that his surreptitious movements had carried to her ears, and he was sorry. He smiled and said, "It's only me." He unsaddled;

she came and stood watching. He handed the gunny sack to her. "Breakfast," he said.

"I was beginning to worry about you," she said.

She went into the shack; when he followed after her, she had bacon sizzling in a frying pan. He crossed over to the bunk and looked at Cory; Cory was still sleeping. He found his carpetbag and fumbled at the catch and dug into the depths of the bag and hauled out a gun and belt and holster. He buckled the belt around his waist.

Marybelle's eyebrows arched. "Has it come to that?"

Ives nodded. "Somebody started shooting again. Next time I'll be able to shoot back."

She put dishes on the table; and as she did so, she glanced toward the bunk. Ives shook his head. "Fix him something you can feed to him," he said. "He's not getting up. Not yet."

"I'll let him sleep as long as he can," she said.

The two of them sat down at the table, and Marybelle passed food to Ives, and she smiled at him then, her smile roguish. She said, "Wouldn't you like it this way every morning?"

He frowned. "I don't want to keep coming to table wearing a gun."

She nodded."I see what you mean. We talked that out last night, didn't we?" She ate in silence, and after she'd poured the coffee she said, "Did you have trouble at Hammer?"

"No one was there but Tana. She fixed the sack for us."

Marybelle pursed her lips. "She knows about Cory being up here? And me?"

Ives nodded.

"That was foolish, Doc," Marybelle said, a trace of anger in her voice. "We'll have Hammer upon us before the day's over."

"You don't know Tana."

"I know women," she countered. "You think a secret's safe with her because you think you've made an appeal to her sentiments. It's you men who are the sentimental ones. A woman will weigh any knowledge for exactly what it's worth. Your Tana's Colonel Carradine's granddaughter, isn't she? She'll see that this chance is too good for the colonel to pass up."

Ives felt the heat grow in him. "Do you think she wants Cory's blood on her hands?"

Marybelle made a face. "She'll talk herself out of that. She'll have herself believing it's for the best. A woman can turn black into white faster than any man could think of doing it."

He put down his coffee cup. "Look," he said, "we've got grub, and we've new dressing for Cory's arm. And we can thank Tana for it!"

"Doc," Marybelle said, "we're quarreling."

She came around the table and stood by him. She lifted a hand to his forehead and brushed away a lock of his hair. She said, "Maybe you're right. I hope you are. She means something to you, doesn't she?"

He said, "I was raised on Hammer."

Cory Lund said, "What the hell is this?"

His eyes were open; his voice was sneering. He lay there in the bunk looking wrung out.

Ives nodded toward him. "Better feed him."

Marybelle moved to prepare a plate. She took it to Cory and lifted a spoon, and Cory said, "Hell, I've got *one* wing." He propped himself on his right elbow, but then he couldn't use the spoon.

"Better let me do it," Marybelle said. Her voice was starchy; her voice dominated Cory. He allowed himself to be fed.

Afterward Ives moved to him. "Let's have a look at that arm."

He kept his thoughts to himself as he examined the wound. It was doing as well as he'd hoped, but some part of his judgment he reserved, even from himself. He called to Marybelle for hot water, and he had a sheet torn into strips and the strips boiled, and later he dressed the wound fresh. Cory watched him always in silence, his eyes hard and his lips drawn down. Cory looked infinitely younger than Marybelle; he looked older than time.

When Ives was finished, Cory glanced at his sister. "You've got a horse? We'll be getting out of here this morning."

Ives said, "You're going to stay where you are. At least today."

Cory said, "I know you're a doctor. And I know she must have fetched you here because there wasn't any other doctor. That doesn't change anything."

Ives said, "Nurse your damn grudge, if you like. But I say you're not going."

"And I say I am!"

Marybelle came to the bunk. "You headstrong fool!" she said. "You'd have lost your arm, but for him. Now quit acting like you ought to be spanked!"

Ives expected Cory to answer her in kind; instead he sank into sullen silence; Ives didn't know which of the two was the older, but he knew now which was the dominant one.

Cory said grudgingly, "I guess I'm beholden to you, Ives. You'll be paid for what you did."

Ives said, "Have you got half a hundred-dollar bill, Cory?"

Cory looked surprised. "I've never seen a hundred-dollar bill in my life."

"Brule backed that play you made in town. He was across the street when you showed up with your two stubble-hopping friends. Afterward Brule laid for me along the road. He had half of a hundred-dollar bill in his pocket."

Cory seemed to turn this over in his mind. "You've got it figured wrong somewhere, Ives. Old Charley was running around town babbling that you were back. I'd heard that Carradine had some sort of stepson, a doctor names Ives. I thought I'd tell you to climb on the stage again. Brule wasn't in on it. If he was across the street, he was taking care of his own business."

Ives said, "Maybe it was him shot you."

"I wouldn't know," Cory said.

Ives frowned thoughtfully. He stood in silence, looking down at Cory; he saw here a petulant youngster who'd had his pride hurt in Tamerlane and would be slow about forgetting that. But he saw, too, a potential ally, and he said then: "Look, Cory, do you really want trouble with Colonel Carradine?"

"I want my people left alone!"

"You wouldn't have helped them if you'd forced me onto that stage. I didn't come to back the colonel with another gun. I came to try to talk him out of his war. That puts us on the same side, doesn't it?"

Cory said, "You'll have to lay more than words on the line."

"Give me time," Ives said.

He walked out of the shack; in the clearing, sunlight lay strong and heavy now, and the woods around the place smelled dry in the daylight. He stood there, one foot upon a stump, his elbow propped upon his knee, his chin cupped in his hand. Marybelle came and stood behind him. She said, "Cory's not a bad kid. He just hasn't really grown up. His way is to kick down anything that stands in front of him."

Ives said, "Would you like to take a ride?"

"With you?"

"Alone. One of us had better stay with Cory. It's your turn now. I'd like you to ride down to your place. Your father will want to know about Cory. And I want to know what's going on down there."

She said, "You're worried."

Ives nodded. "Remember those shots we heard after we rode out of town? That was Hammer trying to snatch me out of jail. The outfit wasn't back at sunup this morning. They may have ridden to the settlement."

"I'll find out about it," she said.

"While you're there, you might ask about those sick children," Ives said. "But just ask. Don't get too close to them."

She gave him a sharp look. "Very well," she said.

She rode away shortly thereafter; when she was gone, he felt a strange loneliness. He paced about the clearing; he looked into the shack and found Cory dozing again. He wondered if Tom Feather were in the vicinity; he'd meant to ask Marybelle if Feather had showed back, but he'd forgotten. He went into the shack again and got his razor from the carpetbag and shaved himself. At noontime he prepared food for himself, then awoke Cory and fed him. Bringing a fresh bucket of water from the well, Ives placed it handy to the bunk.

"If you need anything, holler," he said. "I won't be far off."

"I'll make out," Cory said.

Into the clearing again, Ives idled about and then walked into the woods; the droning sounds of the woods were all about him; at a distance he could hear the gurgle of a creek. He walked toward this creek; it gave him an objective. He was tired and nervous and bored with himself. When he found the creek, he followed it along; soon he heard splashing; he remembered his first meeting with Marybelle and smiled to himself, but this was no swimmer. He became cautious; he made his footfalls light and was glad the gun was at his hip. He took out the weapon and fingered it, then slid it back into the holster. He'd never been very handy with a gun. Soon he came upon Tom Feather squatting beside the creek, a gold pan in his hands. Feather was swirling water in the pan, making a great ritual of this. The old man was completely absorbed.

"Hello," Ives said easily.

Feather looked up with no more than normal surprise. He grunted a greeting and bent his eyes to his work again.

"Any color?" Ives asked.

"Tobacco money, maybe."

Ives paused a moment, wondering what sort of words could build a bridge to this man. Then he made his plunge. "You know a fellow named Jim Ives? Hailed from Texas, I believe."

Feather's face puckered with the effort of thinking. "It's got a familiar sound," he said. "Hell, younker, I'm an old man. I've known a lot of 'em in my time."

"This Ives looked something like me."

Feather peered up at him; Feather seemed to be reaching for something just beyond his fingertips; there was that sort of strained, intent look about him. Then he said, "It's a big crick, mister. I'm kind of busy today."

Ives's despair was not too great; he'd expected this kind of defeat; Tom Feather moved in a different world today than he had last night. Ives said, "Sorry to have bothered you, old-timer."

He turned back to the shack; Cory was awake, but Cory said nothing when he looked in at the door. Ives crossed the clearing again and found a grassy spot among the trees and stretched himself upon the ground, using his hat for a pillow. Above him was the sky, blue and cloudless and remote as anything in the world could be. Ives removed the bandage from about his head. He'd grown tired of that bandage.

He closed his eyes. He'd once heard it propounded that if a man concentrated hard enough he could think himself back to his infancy, and he tried doing this. He had that first memory to go on, cattle lowing beneath a darkling sky. He tried reaching from this memory to others; finally he shaped up a chuck wagon and a fire and men gathered about the fire. He thought harder.

In memory, the colonel came riding up. The colonel sat his horse at the firelight's rim, and a restrained fury was in the man. The colonel began talking, and his anger was because Slash-S cows had crossed the river at the ford and got mixed into the day's gather and now they'd have to be cut out and hazed back. Ives opened his eyes then, disgusted with himself. That had been at a fall roundup here on the Sombra, the first year he'd ridden with the crew. His mind had jumped a span of years from one bunch of cattle to another.

He tried again, but it was hard keeping his mind to the task. Tana got mixed up in his thoughts, not the Tana of long ago, but the Tana of last night, the one who'd surrendered with her lips and then said there could never be any surrender. He tried putting Tana out of his mind and getting back to the real business; and he slept then.

He heard his name called softly. His first consciousness was that time had passed, though it was still daylight. Marybelle was sitting beside him; she'd pulled a blade of grass and was tickling his nose with it. He blew from the corner of his mouth to ease the itch in his nose.

She laughed. She said, "Mostly you look like a grim old man, but when you sleep, you look like a little boy. How old are you, Doc?"

"Old enough to be your great-grandfather," he said. He looked at her. "You had no trouble?"

"I found Dad. He was at our place. I told him about Cory. He sends you his thanks. He said he knew you were a good man."

Ives said, "Then he wasn't oiling a gun?"

She frowned. "There'd been trouble. Hammer shot up Tamerlane last night, then found the jail empty. They rode out to the settlement."

"Yes," he said and drew a long breath.

"They didn't come a-whooping and a-hollering. But they called at every shack. They asked if Rod Benedict was around. It's pretty plain how the colonel figured. If you weren't in Tamerlane, he supposed Benedict had hidden you out, expecting Hammer to raid. What better place to take you than the settlement? But they didn't find Benedict, and they didn't find you. They spent all night looking."

"Benedict was in town," Ives recalled.

"Rod would have been smart enough to lie low when Hammer treed the town."

Ives felt exhilarated. He sat up. He said, "Then the lid wasn't blown off after all. If the colonel had gone slam-banging among the homesteaders, they'd likely have given him a fight. I wonder if he thought of that."

Marybelle leaned and put her arms around him. "Don't you ever have anything but trouble on your mind?"

He stood up, pulling her to her feet. He said, "How about supper?"

"Hell," she said, "you weren't born. You were carved out of ice." But she laughed.

He took her by the hand and they went in this fashion into the clearing and across it to the shack. Marybelle got the fire going; Ives looked into the woodbox and went about filling it. Cory, awake again, kept his sullen silence and watched them. They were at table when Ives heard hoofbeats.

Marybelle heard them, too. She came to a stand, her face white, and made a move toward the door, and Ives said soothingly, "It's just one rider."

"Her!" Marybelle said from the doorway. "I told you you were foolish, Doc. Supposing she's followed?"

Ives was at Marybelle's shoulder; he saw Tana slipping from a horse. Tana wore a divided riding-skirt and a white blouse; a great fear was in her face. She came across the clearing, and Ives brushed past Marybelle and went to meet Tana; and because he could read her desperate urgency, he said at once, "What is it?"

"Rod!" she cried.

"You got to town and got word to him?"

She shook her head; she had ridden hard—the horse showed it—and she was trembling. "Before I could get saddled up this morning, the colonel rode in with the crew. He demanded to know why I was going to town. I couldn't tell him—not unless I told him everything. He refused to let me go."

"He's still at Hammer?"

She nodded. "All day. He sat on the gallery and looked like a man wrestling with the devil. Then Rod came."

"To Hammer?"

"Late this afternoon. He was looking for you. He said you'd broken out of jail."

Ives swore beneath his breath. "The damn fool!" he added aloud, but there was no rancor in it. It was almost as though he had expected this and not realized it; a man who had dared Hammer once would have the nerve to dare it again.

"What happened?" he asked.

"The colonel had the crew get Rod under their guns. He's holding Rod prisoner in the bunkhouse. He says that Rod was bluffing by coming after you, trying to fool us into thinking that the law no longer had you. I couldn't speak up—not without telling him Cory Lund was on Hammer land. The colonel's keeping Rod as hostage, and he's sent word to the nesters. Either they turn you over to Hammer, or Rod stays a prisoner."

Ives said grimly, "We'll straighten that out!"

"If there's time," Tana said, and she was close to weeping. "Brian, don't you see what this will do? What else can the farmers do now but saddle up and come after Rod? And then the lid's off for sure. The colonel's already posted guards at the fence."

Ives opened his hands and closed them. "Hell," he said. "This is the end of everything."

11

Bleak and Bitter Men

IVES STOOD IN THE CLEARING WITH A FEELING OF DEFEAT so strong in him that it brought a sensation of relief, a sensation of being done with impossibles. He had pitted himself against the inevitable ever since his return to this range, and now there would be war. The matter was beyond his changing it. He remembered his thinking of the Sombra as a gigantic chessboard; the pawns had been moved and the play was over. He thought of Oregon and was homesick for Oregon. A man could do only so much.

Tana had a look of infinite tiredness. Tana said, "It's his fool, stiff-backed pride. He's walked in fire ever since Rod took you away from Hammer under his very nose. Being the colonel, he had to hit back."

Ives said dully, "And now he's bringing the whole shebang down about his ears."

Tana said, "Isn't there a chance? I rode as fast as I could, Brian."

He thought: *She rode straight to me*, and in that thought was a challenge that shook the lethargy enfolding him. He said, "I'll get saddled up."

Marybelle had followed Ives into the clearing. Marybelle had heard the talk. Now she pursed her lips; she stood lost in thought for a moment. "I'll ride with you," she said.

He shook his head. "No, it's my turn again. Someone will have to stay with Cory. He's not moving tonight."

Marybelle had a way of suddenly growing older. Again he saw sternness take the sensuality out of her lips, and she said, "I'm going with you!"

He shrugged; in him was a renewed vigor and the cause no longer seemed lost, but he didn't know how to go about pitting himself against Marybelle, and he sensed that he never would. He turned to Tana. "Could you stay with Lund till we get back?"

Tana shrugged, showing no real interest. "If you wish, Brian."

Marybelle said, "Doc, will you never get it through your head that there are two sides to any fence?"

Something rose in Tana's eyes that was the ghost of the colonel. She said quietly, "I won't poison him."

One girl looked at the other, Ives standing between them, and neither let belligerency show; it was eye matched against eye and both gazes holding steadily; and he had no understanding of this kind of warfare, but he could feel the force of it. Marybelle was taking a careful measure of Tana, and Ives judged that the run of Marybelle's thoughts was stormy, but Marybelle said then, as quietly as Tana had spoken, *"I'll* stay with Cory."

Color came to Tana's cheeks as if she had been slapped by an invisible hand. She said, "Very well," and her unconcern made it her victory.

Ives was impatient with all this. He got the saddle and gear and flung it upon the horse and climbed into the kak. Cory Lund shaped up in the shack's doorway; he stood there unsteady, and Ives said, "Get back to your bunk!"

Cory said, "I heard. Big trouble's in the wind. I'm riding out."

Here was meat for the kind of ax Ives could swing, and he said, "You're getting back to that bunk, if I have to tie you. I didn't save that arm to have you running around getting it infected!"

Cory said, "The hell with my arm!"

Ives said, "What good will it do to have one more hothead loose? You get inside."

Marybelle said, "You're burning time, Doc. I'll take care of him."

Ives turned to Tana. "Come on," he said and Tana mounted and they rode through the timber to a game trail. They started descending; the narrowness of the trail kept them in single file. Dusk gathered the hills in its shadowy arms; the night came unobtrusively, and soon they were down out of the deeper timber and among stunted trees, the range spreading before them, and the lights of Tamerlane twinkling distantly.

Then Tana said, "You're not heading to Hammer?"

Ives shook his head. "The colonel's holding Benedict and standing pat. That makes the next move up to the nesters. If the trouble's to be stopped, it has to be stopped first at the settlement."

Tana said, "Then it would have been better if the Lund girl had come along."

They were riding stirrup to stirrup; he turned and saw the solemn gravity of her face. He said, "You two just don't like each other, do you? Why is that?"

She said in surprise, "Don't you know, Brian?"

Irritation edged his voice. "There's a very great deal I don't know!" His thought was that this was the way of women; given a real war, they would keep it second to their own petty warfare; given a clean-cut issue, they preferred to deal in obscurities. He had no patience with this, and he said, "Marybelle made her choice. I'll get along without her tonight."

Tana said, "She's very worth while, Brian."

She put a sincerity into this that melted him. He looked at her again; he saw that worry had ravaged her, and he searched a way to soothe her. He said, "You don't need to fret about Rod. The colonel won't harm him. When it comes to a last ditch, the colonel will remember that Rod wears a badge. And he'll also remember that Rod once rode for Hammer."

Tana said, "I can't help worrying."

Ives swept his arm toward Hammer. "Can you make it alone from here?"

"I'll ride with you," she said.

He frowned. "I don't know what's waiting down at the settlement."

"I'll ride with you," she said again.

He had no time for arguing. He said, "Very well," and looked toward the Sombra. He could pick out the distant pinpoints of light that marked the nester settlement, and these became his beacon. He was not too familiar with the lie of the land for he had come here in darkness last night. They moved along; he kept his eyes upon the lights; the lights grew larger. The two came upon fences which they had to follow to gates; the fences were a regular maze. Marybelle had known how to avoid the fences last night. Ives chafed at the delay and wished Marybelle were along again.

Soon the horses rustled through corn patches, and dogs barked at them, and at last he and Tana rode into a yard before the first of the tar-paper shacks. This yard was gray with flung dishwater; a tin washtub hung from the wall beside the door. Light showed in the windows; and when Ives halloed, the door opened and a woman stood framed, a child tugging at her skirts.

Ives said, "I'm looking for Elisha Lund's place."

The woman said, "Down a piece farther," and waved her arm to the south. Her face was inflexible; her face shut him out from further talk. The door closed with a solid finality, and he realized then that Tana's horse bore Hammer's brand upon its shoulder.

They were to stop at several of these strung-out places within the hour; always there was the woman, always there was the wave to the south; and this became a changeless routine until they found the woman with a different fear in her face. She stood hesitantly in the door of her shack and gave the directions, and then she looked at the black garb of Ives and said, "You'd be the doctor?"

"Yes," he said.

"If you could look at my young one—"

He realized then that this was Jensen's place where last night he'd watched a man walk to and fro. His impulse was to step down from the saddle, but he remembered the tangle of fences and all the lost time. Always there had to be first things first. "I'll be back as soon as I can," he promised.

The woman said, "I'll be obliged."

When they were riding again, Tana said, "Have you noticed that we haven't found a man at any of the places?"

"Yes," he said, his mouth drawing grim. "I've noticed."

Shortly thereafter they saw the fire.

Fear held Ives in the first moment; that fire was big enough to be a shack burning; and his thought was that the colonel hadn't stood pat, the colonel had brought the war to the settlement. He remembered Marybelle's talk of last night, her memory of lumbering along in a wagon and not looking back because her home was burning. He jogged his horse; Tana pressed hers harder, keeping abreast of him. Soon Ives saw that the fire stood in the openness between a shack and the scattered outbuildings of Elisha Lund's place. About this fire, men stood massed in ragged ranks, bleak and bitter men, and the firelight danced upon rifle barrels; and the high gauntness of Lund stood outlined.

Tana held back then, checking her horse.

Into the rim of the firelight Ives rode boldly; Lund had been talking, his voice a reaching rumble that fell to nothing as Ives shaped up, and silence came down hard and held all these men, the sound of a snapping stick in the fire's heart loud in that silence. This was the way of the first moment—silence and a startled recognition and a beating animosity that rose in the night and settled upon Ives. He carefully wrapped his reins around the saddle horn and sat his saddle. He found that his palms were moist, and he ran them along his thighs.

He said, "Good evening, Lund," singling out the man because, of them all, Lund was the only one he might possibly call friend.

Lund's hard-planed features showed astonishment, but he said, "Good evening," with that trace of Scandinavian accent that made it, "Goot evening."

Ives said, "Cory's doing fine. Just fine."

Lund said, "That's goot." He hesitated; Ives could see that there was in this situation much that defied Lund's usual directness. Lund said, "Marybelle told me. I'm much obliged."

Ives said, "I'm on my way to Hammer. The colonel will be turning Benedict loose when he realizes you fellows aren't holding me. I dropped by to tell you that if you'll give me a few hours, I'll have your sheriff back."

He felt more at ease now; he felt that he had won Lund by that reference to Cory and the work that had been done on Cory, but he was aware of the gun strapped around his waist, and he wished he'd left it behind. They were eyeing that gun. He could almost reach out and touch the temper of these men, and their temper was uncertain. He was Hammer in their minds. Feet stirred restlessly, and there was much shifting of rifles, and he saw scowls and wooden blankness.

Then somebody said, "He's a damn spy for Hammer!"

Ives said, "You're wrong, friend."

Others took voice; their words were a babel with only the tone to be perceived, and that tone held suspicion and open antagonism. But above this Lund's voice rumbled.

"Let him have his say," Lund ordered; this was the coin in which a doctor got his payment.

"I've had my say," Ives said. "I'm riding to Hammer. I'm only asking you fellows to wait till I come back. What difference whether you have your war tonight or tomorrow, if war it's got to be? I tell you I'll bring Benedict back to you!" He appealed to Lund. "Haven't you told them why I've been missing? The colonel doesn't know I broke jail. And I couldn't have sent word to him without letting him know where Cory is."

Lund plucked at his yellow beard, his eyes troubled. He looked toward the massed men. "Jorgensen," he said, "tell him what you told us when you got back today."

A man moved in the crowd. He was young and big and thick-shouldered, and his face held no compromise. He looked at Ives and spat into the fire. He said, "I was down to the railroad this week. The telegraph operator there, he's a cousin of mine. He said Colonel Carradine sent a wire not long ago. To Cheyenne. For all the gunmen that would hire out to Hammer. He wanted them as fast as they could come."

Ives said desperately, "He won't have any call for gunmen unless you fellows ride against Hammer."

Anger brightened Jorgensen's eyes. "You want us to stall for another day or two. Then maybe his gunmen will get here. I'm thinking that's why he sent you."

The voices rose again, the mingled voices; and Ives saw then upon what their suspicion was based, and he remembered that Marco Stoll had told him that Carradine was making open talk of importing gunmen. No denial could have any teeth in it, not in the face of the news Jorgensen had fetched, and Ives said, "A few hours. Just a few hours. That's all I ask!"

Jorgensen detached himself from the group and skirted the fire, coming to a stand at the shoulder of Ives's horse. He reached a mighty hand and wrapped it in Ives's coat and yanked. Jorgensen said, "You damn spy! Come off that horse and take a beating!"

Ives sliced at Jorgensen's wrist with the edge of his own right hand. "Take your paw off me!"

Elisha Lund said sharply, "None of that!" and Jorgensen's hand fell away, but the man stood there, anger smoldering in his eyes. Jorgensen looked around him and said, "I say keep him here while we've got him. That gives us him to stack up against Rod Benedict."

Ives looked at Lund; Lund owed him something now, and Lund was his only hope. But Lund was more than Cory's father, Lund was the leader of these men; and therefore Lund would be making no compromise, in spite of a bit of lead that had tinkled in a dishpan.

Lund still plucked at his beard. He said, "I don't know. I yoost don't know."

Tana nudged her horse into the firelight. "You want a hostage," she said. "I'll be your hostage."

Ives judged that they hadn't seen her till now; she had held back, he supposed, because it was a man's place to do the talking. She sat now in the firelight's glow; the firelight touched her face and found it impassive; and the silence came down again until the voices broke into an astonished babble. Ives had to smile, wondering if she had timed her appearance to wring this drama out of it. But he turned and said, "This isn't your play, Tana."

She said, "I'm giving them a bargain, if they want one."

He looked at her, admiration in his eyes, and he said, "I wonder if Benedict knows how lucky he is!"

But Tana was looking at Lund. "You know me," she said. "I'll make you a better ace in the hole than Doctor Ives. Let him go."

Lund had little defense against this. He said, "This is man's business."

In Tana now was a princess's haughtiness, and in this moment she dominated all of them, and Ives thought of the ways of women and marveled. No man here counted himself less than her equal, and the power that she held was as nameless as it was potent. Possibly it came from breeding—a farmer could understand breeding. Possibly it was the colonel's blood in her that made her dominant; the colonel would have sat like this, staring them down.

Tana said, with just a shade of scorn, "Don't you men even take a chance when you've got everything on your side?"

Lund's eyes puckered, laughter wrinkles forming around them, but he kept his lips stiff. He spoke to Ives. "You're riding one of my horses," Lund said. "I'll get you a fresh one. You'd better get back here mighty fast."

Ives frowned at Tana. "I didn't want this kind of an out," he said.

She said low-voiced, "Get moving. Get moving before they change their minds. I'm as safe here as I'd be on Hammer."

He turned to Lund. "Snake out that horse. I'll be back by morning."

He came down from the saddle; and Jorgensen stepped back, his face blank and his hands hanging limply; and only then was Ives sure that Tana had won for him.

12

The Key

IVES WENT AT HAMMER AS THE CROW FLIES, MAKING A straight line from Lund's place eastward and holding the horse to a good steady pace. Behind him lay half a victory—that was Tana's doing—and the desperate urgency that had goaded him on the trail to the settlement was no longer so sharp a spur. He felt almost gay; he felt big enough to move a mountain. He was Rod Benedict's key to freedom, and this the colonel couldn't deny. The rest of his mission would be automatic, and thereafter the colonel would have to call quits or turn his hand to some fresh folly. Then Ives remembered Jorgensen's report about the telegram to Cheyenne and frowned. The colonel had lighted a fuse with that telegram. What good could come of delaying the inevitable explosion?

The night misted up and a little rain came, no more than a soft drizzle; Ives turned up his shirt collar and wished he hadn't left his Prince Albert at Feather's place. The rain obscured the range and made footing uncertain; the rain darkened his mood further, washing the last of his high feelings out of him, and futility became his saddle mate. He remembered the fire at Lund's place, and the light of it dancing upon gun barrels; he recalled Carradine's stubbornness when they'd talked on Hammer's gallery, and he felt himself pulled one way and another in a tug of war which was no real concern of his. Again he felt homesick for Oregon. Then he thought of Tana.

She'd be seated in Elisha Lund's house now, waiting out the hours. She'd be the recipient of a strange, stiff courtesy, a princess held hostage by serfs, but her hope would be high—her hope would be in Brian Ives. He remembered what Marybelle had said about women narrowing their needs to essentials. Tana knew that war was coming. But out of tonight Tana would get Rod Benedict safe away from Hammer, and there would be that much accomplished. Ives had been thinking in the larger sense, and therein lay the futility. Now there was something to be done that made its own difference in at least two lives. He pressed onward.

The rain had slackened off to nothing when he hit Hammer's fence, and the moon broke through the overcast and laid feeble light on the barbed-wire strands. Ives began following the fence toward the gate, but whenever the moon lost itself, he lost the fence. He began using matches, chafing at the delay. Then he found himself upon a road, and when he gave the horse its head, the horse followed the road. It came to Ives that this was the road the nesters used to take them to Tamerlane; farther down, it forked into Hammer's road. A nester horse would know a nester road, so he let the mount pick its own way. He might lose a mile or two by this method, but if he watched for the fork and turned there, he was bound to come to Hammer's gate.

When the moon showed itself again and he had a look at the surrounding country, he found that he had veered far away from the fence, but he was unconcerned; the surest way was the quickest way. He rode at a lively trot, and when he reached the fork he saw a buggy coming up out of the south, a square box buggy, and he knew it instantly. He would remember that buggy always; he was sure his fingermarks were in its top supports; he had ridden that buggy in agony, with Marybelle at the reins. He hauled his horse to a halt and waited; the buggy came up and stopped. It had rained harder farther south; mud fell from the wheels.

Marco Stoll said, "Man! Where have you been keeping yourself?"

Stoll was alone in the buggy; he filled the seat and sagged its cushion, and when he leaned from the buggy and the moonlight touched him, his full round face had a strange bleakness. The joviality was gone out of him. He said sharply, "How did you get out of jail?"

Irritation touched Ives, and he had to remind himself that he owed something to this man; he owed Stoll twice for friendship, once displayed by a shotgun from a window and again displayed in the weed-choked lot next to Tamerlane's jail. These things must be weighed against the suspicion he'd known and dismissed when he'd thought of Sombra Range as a chessboard on which some unseen hand manipulated the pawns. He said, "I left the jail with the Lund girl. She'd found Cory; he wasn't dead. But he needed a doctor."

"Hammer hit the town with the idea of grabbing you," Stoll said. "They came just a little late."

"I know." Ives looked impatiently northward. "I'd better be riding. What brings you out on a night like this?"

"I'm heading for the settlement. The word's got to town that the lid's about to blow off. What fool business is this, the colonel holding Benedict?"

"He's hostage for me. I'm on my way to make the swap."

Stoll's face grew reflective. Incongruously, he said, "I thought I noticed a bandage on your head when Benedict fetched you in the other day. I meant to ask about that when I came to the jail."

"I got shot on my way to Hammer that first day."

"Shot!"

"Brule did it."

"Brule? Why should he hate you that much?"

"It was a job of work for somebody else."

Stoll's rubbery lips shaped to whistle, but they made no sound. He looked dazed. He said, "And still you stick on this range!"

Ives said bluntly, "You're buying into trouble, too."

"I'm going to the settlement to try talking those fool farmers into thinking twice before they start the fireworks. What good would a war be to anybody?"

Ives said, "You were a cattleman once, weren't you? Aren't you heading the wrong way?"

Stoll shrugged. "Why ride a horse that gets too old to ride? I told you this is going to be sodbuster country. I've got a stake here; you haven't. You've been shot at, and you might have been lynched. How much medicine do you have to take. Doc, before it gags you? I gave you a piece of advice once; it still holds. This road leads back to Tamerlane. You're too late for tonight's stage, but there'll be one tomorrow. You can bed down in my quarters, if you like." He began probing his pockets. "I've got the key here somewhere."

Ives laughed. "I'm the key—the key to the whole thing tonight. Lund's waiting for Rod Benedict to come riding back. There's going to be war if he doesn't."

"It's coming anyway, Doc. I'm driving to the Sombra, yes, but a fat lot of good it will do. But if I was an outsider, I'd be taking the stage."

Ives said, "Thanks just as much."

Anger mastered Stoll; it writhed in his face before it broke its bonds, and he said then, explosively, "You're a fool!"

"Yes," Ives said, "I'm a fool." He drew his horse aside. "I'm in your way."

Stoll's face vanished into the shadow beneath the buggy's top; he slapped the reins against his horse's back, and the buggy jerked forward. Ives watched it go; in him was the feeling that he had somehow tried Stoll's patience too sorely and made an enemy tonight. He wondered at the man's strange persistence as regarded himself; he could find no sense in it, and it troubled him. The buggy was taking the fork toward the Sombra; Ives shrugged and headed north along the main road. He had no time for riddles tonight, and Stoll was a riddle.

He reached Hammer's gate not long after; men moved dimly in the shadows beyond, and he hadn't realized how easily he might have died, approaching thus. Hammer was alert; Hammer was ready for whatever the night might hold, and this kind of alertness could have a hair-trigger to it. A voice lifted in the night saying, "Sing out, you!"

He reined short. "It's me—Ives."

The voice beyond the gate said, less truculently, "Where the devil have you been?" The gate creaked open, and Ives rode through. At least three men were here; he could make out that many. He said, "The colonel at the ranch?"

"He's up there."

Ives rode on; he came to the avenue of cottonwoods and lost himself in the shadows; he had a sense of men all around him; the tenseness of Hammer was a living thing. He came upon the buildings and was surprised that no light showed in the ranch house and very little in the bunkhouse. Men stirred about, keeping their voices low. Ives left the horse in the yard, the reins looped around the banister of the steps climbing to the gallery; he loosened the cinch but didn't unsaddle, and then he walked toward the bunkhouse. A man shaped up before him; he knew this one from other days. He said, "Where's the colonel, Harry?"

"Bedded down," Harry said. He was a man grown gray in the service of Hammer; he had always been sparse of words. Some truculence born of tension was in him now.

"Benedict here?"

"Yonder," Harry said and inclined his head toward the bunkhouse.

Ives stepped to the bunkhouse window. He said, "Rod," very low, and Benedict's boyish face framed itself in the window. Benedict looked tight-lipped and worn, like a man who'd wrung all the juices out of his anger; leaving only its solid core. But he grinned when he recognized Ives.

Benedict said, "It comes to me that the last time it was the other way around. Then I was the one on the outside looking in. Where you been keeping yourself, feller?"

Ives said, "We've got a ride to make and time to do our talking then. I'm here to get you out."

Benedict said, "Who told you about me?"

Ives said, "Tana," saying it with his lips only and not making any carrying sound, and the change that came over Benedict was worth this night's riding. The anger in Benedict melted; his face grew gentle. Ives walked to the door of the bunkhouse and found it padlocked. The padlock was used when all the crew was gone upon roundup; tonight it made a jail out of the bunkhouse. Ives turned angrily. "Harry," he said, "unlock this thing!"

Harry said, "Colonel's got the key." Two or three others had come drifting up. They formed a solid group behind Harry, they were a rock.

Ives said, "The colonel was holding him till I came back. Well, I'm here. I want him turned loose."

Harry said, "You'll have to see the colonel about that." He spat. "Hell, I ain't got nothin' against the kid."

Ives stepped to the window again. "Rod," he said, "I'll be back in a minute."

"Take your time," Benedict said. "Take your own sweet time."

In Ives was a slow anger, but it burned itself out before he reached the gallery. He knew the iron hand that ruled Hammer; he had felt that hand in the past, and he couldn't blame Harry for another man's obstinacy. He reached the door; last night he'd knocked upon it, but tonight he put his hand to the latch, and the door gave to his touch. He walked into the big main room, and the memory of Tana and last night was in this room, and the memory rose and was all around him, softening him. He groped past the table with the piled magazines; he had a map of the house in his mind, and recalling where the colonel's bedroom was, he edged toward it.

Into this room, he paused, trying to get his eyes used to the darkness; the banjo clock clattered on the wall. The colonel was in bed; he could make out the colonel's white hair. He called the man's name softly; Carradine had always been a light sleeper, but he didn't stir. Ives wondered then if the colonel were feigning sleep, and his anger renewed itself.

He felt about the room and found a chair with the colonel's black suit laid neatly upon it; he found the trousers and groped through the pockets for the key to the padlock. He drew a perverse pleasure from the thought of taking Benedict from the bunkhouse and the colonel not finding out until morning. But the key wasn't in the colonel's trousers.

He reached for the coat, feeling into its pockets and exploring their farthest corners, and his fingers touched paper. The paper had the feel of money; he ran his thumb along the edge and found one edge jagged; and then, suddenly, he was sick. He didn't want to believe what his fingers told him; he drew forth the paper and held it in one hand and dug into his own pockets for a match. He snapped the match aflame with his thumbnail and looked at the paper.

The colonel said calmly, distinctly, "Have you stooped to picking pockets, sir?"

Ives tried looking toward the colonel, but the match had blinded him; he had the impression that the colonel had propped himself up on one elbow. Ives let the match go out, and he said in the darkness, "I always knew that you hated me. But I never knew how much."

The colonel said, "Just what is that gibberish supposed to mean?"

Ives said, "You know what it means," and he made a fist out of his left hand and folded the piece of paper in his fist, the torn half of a hundred-dollar bill, the half that matched the half Brule had carried in his pocket the day he'd waited atop a cutbank for a traveler along Hammer's road. And then, remembering that the colonel had always slept with a loaded forty-five beneath his pillow, Ives took a quick sideward step, trying to make of himself a hard target to find.

13

Tail of the Trail

IN THIS MOMENT WHEN ALL OF IVES'S CONCEPTION OF Carradine stood changed, his first feeling was shock, and out of this came a woodenness of mind that made his thinking clumsy, leaving him only instinct. The colonel had wanted him dead; therefore danger dwelt here, and the danger was Carradine, who had suddenly become an enemy. These things clamored in Ives's mind, not separately but as a sum total; instinct drove deeper—the instinct to survive. He got his gun into his hand; he strained his eyes against the darkness; and he said, low-voiced, "I know you keep a gun handy. Make a move for it and I'll start shooting!"

Carradine said, "Have you gone completely insane, sir?"

His voice was firm; it held the old authority, that and a certain bewilderment; and because the bewilderment was genuine, Ives's conviction was slightly shaken. Or was this a ruse of the colonel's, born of desperation? Ives thought: *Doesn't he realize that I know?* He said, "The time's past for bluffing. I was looking for the key to the bunkhouse. I found the other half of the hundred-dollar bill."

Carradine said, "Would you mind explaining the significance of that bill?" His voice was cool; it held the petulant patience of a parent reasoning with a stubborn child, and again his bewilderment was genuine.

Ives said, "Brule had the other half. The day he shot me from the cutbank."

The colonel drew in his breath, and silence held for a long moment, the steady beat of the banjo clock becoming a clamor. Then the colonel said, "Would you light a lamp?"

Ives thought first that here was a ruse to relax his wariness, and his instinct was to refuse. Then he grew angry with himself; oddly, though he had feared this man all of his days, now that he had the greatest reason to fear him, he had found contempt, and that mastered the fear. He groped toward a bureau standing against one wall, found a lamp, and fumbled for a match and scraped it aglow. But instead of touching it to the lamp, he held the flame high; his contempt was tempered by that much wariness. The colonel had not moved; the colonel was still propped up on an elbow, his silvery hair tousled, his aristocratic face troubled.

Ives laid his gun on the dresser top and lifted the chimney of the lamp with his right hand and touched the match to the wick. He adjusted the wick and turned toward the colonel again, leaving the gun.

The colonel said, "One of the crew went to town for the mail the other day. There was an envelope addressed to me in a fist that had been made to appear a childish scrawl. That torn half of a bill was inside—nothing more. The envelope was postmarked Tamerlane that very day. I wasted little consideration on anything so senseless. I put the bill in my pocket."

Ives said slowly, "I don't believe you."

The banked fire behind the colonel's blue eyes blazed for an instant, and then he shrugged. "Doubtless I wouldn't believe it myself, if our positions were reversed."

Ives said, "You must have found out that Tana had sent for me. Didn't you give half that bill to Brule, intending to give him the other half when his work was done? Or are you trying to imply that the person who hired Brule mailed that bill to you on the thousand-to-one chance that I'd find it in your pocket?"

"You knew that Brule had half the bill," Carradine said. "Did he know that you knew it?"

Ives nodded.

"Then Brule could have told the man who held the other half."

"And that man mailed it to you?" Ives shook his head. "That would be too long a chance."

Again Carradine shrugged. "A man fires in the dark. If he misses his mark, he's wasted his lead. But there's always the chance that he may hit. Supposing I'd showed you the bill and told you how I'd come by it? Wouldn't you have been just as suspicious?"

Ives passed the back of his hand across his forehead. "I don't know what to think," he said. "There's more than the finding of the bill. I had to tack that onto all the things that never made sense to me—your coldness toward me when I was a boy, your coldness toward my coming back to this range."

Carradine said, "But why should I want you dead?"

"That," Ives said, "is what I don't know. All I know is that when I walk out of this house tonight, I'll never come back."

Carradine looked at him in the lamplight; Carradine's eyes grew reflective, the eyes of a man doing his own desperate sort of weighing. He said at last, "Then the time has come to tell you."

He flung back the covers and brought his lean legs to the floor; his feet fumbled for slippers and thrust into them, and he stood up. He wore a long white nightgown; another man might have looked ridiculous in it. He crossed to the bureau and lifted the lamp and his shadow flung itself across the floor and angled up the wall. He said, "In here," and led the way to the big book-lined room. He set the lamp upon the centering table and waved Ives toward the sofa. "Sit down."

"I'll stand," Ives said. He'd taken the gun from the bureau before he'd followed the colonel. He thrust the gun into its holster and folded his arms.

The colonel took a chair. The colonel said, "I don't suppose you remember Texas?" Ives shook his head, and the colonel said, "You were born there. You were about two when you came north. That was twenty-three years ago."

Ives said, "Yes?"

Carradine's eyes closed; he leaned back in the chair and his voice dropped. "A lot of us were leaving Texas; the graze had thinned out and we had gone looking for new range. That's history of a sort, and I suppose you know it. Some like John Chisum headed into New Mexico. Some like Goodnight went to Colorado. We didn't believe at first that stock could winter in Montana, but we discovered we were wrong. My boy, Dave, rode up here and scouted this range and built the first dwelling on Hammer."

Ives started. "Tana's father?"

"Tana's father." The colonel's voice trailed away; the colonel looked back across the years and his face turned bitter. "Tana was born here; that was why she was named Montana. Dave left his little family in the north and came back to Texas to report, and we got ready for the big move. We threw our herd in with a neighbor's who was also trailing north." He opened his eyes. "A widower named Jim Ives."

Ives said, "My father. I guessed that much from something Tom Feather said."

Carradine nodded. "We put both herds under the same road brand. And we headed them north—"

He paused; again his words pained him; Ives could see that. The colonel held silent, and that left the picture for Ives to complete for himself, but he had known Texas men all of his days; he had heard of the great migration. Dust and noise; the shouting of men and the clatter of horn and hoof as the longhorns had been flushed from the thickets and shaped into trail herds. Ropes popping and chuck wagons creaking, and the remembered names from forgotten campfires—Rocks Bluff ford and Colbert's Ferry and Kiamichi Valley. Spanish fever and irate Kansas grangers guarding their borders with ready shotguns. The great rivers—the Red, the Cimarron, the Canadian—horns tossed above racing waters, and the nameless graves on the far banks. Bedded cattle in the starshine and the coyote's lonely cry, and the night herders' voices staving off stampede: "Git along, little dogies, for you know Montana will be your new home—"

Somewhere in that migration lay the riddle of all of his days. And now that door long closed was about to be opened, and Ives felt an unsteadiness within himself, felt a need to sit down, but still he stood.

"We had trouble in the Nations," Carradine's voice suddenly droned. "Trail wolves hit at us and some men died, and after that suspicion was born. One among us took long rides at night, and the suspicion was that he was an intimate of the men who'd struck at the herd. Finally we put him on trail. He was Jim Ives's segundo, a man of doubtful antecedents. I think that you call him friend. Marco Stoll."

"Stoll!" Ives said and remembered that Stoll had been a cowboy, but still there was no fitting Stoll into this tale of the colonel's.

Anger edged the colonel's voice. "I was for tipping up a wagon tongue and hanging him. Dave was of the same mind. We were equally convinced of his guilt. But still the evidence was flimsy. Jim Ives pleaded for Stoll, and what Jim lacked in eloquence he made up in sincerity, and when the vote was taken it was decided that Stoll would be punished and banished. I named the punishment. Fifty lashes with him tied to a wagon wheel."

"Stoll!" Ives said again, and Stoll turned leaner and younger in his mind and stood spread-eagled against the wheel, his wrists lashed and the whip rising and falling, the campfire lighting the scene, and the bedded herd out upon the flats blackness against blackness.

"We drew straws to see who'd mete out the punishment. And now I shall show you irony. The man who'd argued for Stoll's life was the man who drew the short straw. Jim Ives laid on with the whip, and Stoll was sent stumbling into the night."

Ives thought of Tamerlane's street and Cory Lund facing him, and the shotgun of Marco Stoll intimidating Lund; he thought of this and of Stoll speaking to him through the jail window; and he thought then that that stranger, Jim Ives, who had been his father, had bequeathed him one thing—Stoll's friendship. And yet he wondered, recalling Stoll's anger tonight.

He said, "So that's why Stoll was told never to set foot on Hammer."

"He came to Tamerlane after the town was built. He stunk with money and he'd grown too fat for riding, so he opened a drugstore. Somewhere in the years between Texas and Montana, he'd learned that business. It has always been my belief that his money came from raided herds, and though he's shown no animosity toward me, I've wanted no part of Marco Stoll. The man is a thief."

Ives remembered the fifty lashes and said, "He took the medicine of one, anyway."

Carradine closed his eyes again. "That should have been the end of it, the whipping and his going in the night. But it was only the beginning of trouble that grew between Dave and Jim Ives, and always there was talk of whether justice or injustice had been meted out. They were both young; they were both hotheaded; I've tried to remember that, and to remember, too, that the trail shortened men's tempers. But there was a night when they drew guns and only the crew's quickness kept them from shooting each other. As it was, a couple of bullets flew."

A thin hand rose, and Carradine touched the scar upon his forehead, and Ives knew now how the colonel had come by that scar.

Carradine said, "The next day we divided the herd and Jim Ives went his separate way."

And now there came back to Ives that fretful night with the bedded herd lowing and two men facing each other across a fire, temper in them, the violence bubbling high and spilling over, and he knew then where his fear had had its beginning. Always when cattle lowed, the fear had come back, but now it had a meaning to it and was banished, and he felt strangely free for the first time in his days.

Carradine said, "We stopped at Dodge. We'd seen no town since we'd left Texas, so we planned to rest for a day. Jim Ives had got there the night before. I don't suppose you remember Dodge City."

Remember? There was the campfire talk again, the tall tales of Texas men, and so the old names rang in Ives's mind—Front Street and Boot Hill and Hell's Half Acre and the Lone Star dance hall. Texas men crowding their horses into the plaza where the glassed-in coal-oil lamps spread their brilliance. Barrels of water placed along the street in case of fire—barbershops—soft-spoken marshals—a preacher's voice raised in a saloon, raised in the old hymns.

"I'm not sure," Ives said.

"We gave our men part of their pay on the flats of the Arkansas and drew straws again, this time to see who'd stay with the herd while the others visited Dodge. Some men wanted whiskey and some wanted cards and some wanted women. But Dave had a different desire. He was a man with a wife and a child waiting for him in Montana. All he wanted was to know how it felt to sleep in a bed, after those nights on the trail. He rode into Dodge to get a hotel room. He got one. He never came out of it alive."

Ives said, "Marco Stoll?"

"No," Carradine said. "Jim Ives."

In the silence the lamp's flames seemed to sob in its chimney, and the old scar stood out upon Carradine's forehead, and his voice was brittle with pain. "One of my crew dropped in at the hotel to pass a word or two with Dave that night," he said. "Tom Feather. There were guns, and the sound of them drew the marshal of Dodge to Dave Carradine's room. He found Dave dead, a gun in his hand, and Jim Ives dead, and Tom Feather shot to doll ribbons. Feather never recovered from that night, so we never knew the whole truth. But we pieced it out after making inquiries. Ives came looking for Dave, and of course he came with anger in him. Feather must have sided with Dave."

Ives said, "And that's how I came to Hammer?"

"With Ives dead, his crew had nothing to do but drift," the colonel said. "That left a two-year-old child with nobody's care. I took you. Yes, that's how you came to Hammer. And that's why you grew up here. I took Jim Ives's herd on with me. It paid for your support."

Ives said, "But all the while you've hated me."

Carradine said, "I've tried to be stronger than that. You had no part in what happened in Dodge. But if you ever want to see Jim Ives's picture, look in any mirror. Every time I've looked at you, I've seen Jim Ives alive and Dave Carradine dead."

Ives said slowly, "And Tana knew." And now he understood the things she'd left wordless last night, and now he knew that she was lost to him forever.

"Your father and hers," Carradine said.

Ives sat down. He put his elbows upon his knees and his face in his hands. He sat like this for a long time, and then he said, "I'll be going now. I owe you more than I owe any man. I'll never trouble you again."

Carradine said, "There's still that matter of the torn hundred-dollar bill."

Ives said, "Who sent it to you?"

Carradine made a gesture with his hands. "How should I know? The nesters, perhaps. They probably supposed you came home to help me. It's an old device, dividing the enemy."

Ives shook his head. "Elisha Lund isn't a subtle man. It was someone else." He paused, the name came to him without his bidding. "Stoll?"

"Perhaps Stoll hates me," Carradine said. "But he has no reason to hate you. Or was Brule waiting for me? He could have fired at you in the anger of the moment."

Ives said, "I don't know."

Carradine looked at Ives; Carradine was his old imperious self, and he said, "I've told you the truth about what happened on the trail so that your judgment of me can be honest. Yes, I despise the name of Ives. But I do my own gunning."

Ives said, "Then we've finished with our talk. I came for the key to the bunkhouse. There's no reason for you to hold Benedict."

Carradine said, "Perhaps *I* might play at dividing the enemy. I've got Benedict; I could keep him."

"Tana's at Elisha Lund's," Ives said. "She offered to be hostage until Benedict was returned."

Carradine said, "Tana!" and his scar flamed. "Are they using women as weapons, sir?"

"It was Tana's choice," Ives said. He extended his hand. "The key?"

Carradine stood up, his nightgown flapping about his ankles. He walked from the room and Ives heard a bureau drawer creak open. The colonel returned, the key in his hand; he gave the key to Ives. The colonel said, "Tell Harry I said to let him go." The colonel mustered fierceness, but it was hollow. "Be damned sure that Tana gets back here safely!"

Ives said, "I will," and started for the door. He took a last glance back; Carradine was standing in the center of the room, his hands before him and his face empty, like a man stricken blind.

14

Back to the Sombra

THEY SAW THE SOMBRA IN THE FIRST DAYLIGHT, THE TWO of them, and here they rested their saddles after the long ride from Hammer; and Rod Benedict angled a leg around his saddle horn and fished out the makings. He built a smoke and offered Durham and papers to Ives, but Ives shook his head. He favored a pipe. Benedict got the tobacco burning and looked less tense than he had. He said, "I never really felt safe, not even when we passed through the gate. The colonel isn't going to be happy about this." He looked at Ives. "You're a glum-looking specimen this fine morning, Doc."

Ives said, "We'd better move on."

Benedict frowned; the frown took the boyishness out of him and gave him a grave maturity. "Must be you bucked the colonel to get that bunkhouse unlocked," he said. "That couldn't have been easy. I'm beholden to you."

Ives looked toward the river; the first light was like smoke upon the waters. Ives's face was bleak with his thinking; his face was dead. He had been rootless for a long, long time, but not like this, not with the last tie cut.

He said, "You can do something for me, Rod, when you get the chance. You can lay your hands on Brule. I want to talk to that gentleman. I want very much to talk to him."

Benedict nodded. "You'll get that chance."

He dropped his leg to the stirrup; both men jogged their horses and moved westward. They came within the hour to Lund's place, and the ground was black where the fire had burned itself out last night, and there were not so many men about; though some had remained. They stood in the yard; they sat upon chopping-blocks; they leaned against the corral. None of them had slept, Ives supposed, and fatigue gave them an added sullenness. They showed interest as the pair rode up, but there was no wild excitement. They moved slowly toward the two horsemen, and Ives said wearily, not lifting his voice, "Here's your badge-toter."

Elisha Lund came to the door of his shack. He had his look and raised one huge hand and let it drop, and he smiled then, but it was a melancholy smile.

Ives said, "I fetched him, Lund."

Tana appeared behind Lund. She looked handsome; she held to her steady serenity, but her eyes were glad. Benedict looked hard at her and stepped down from the saddle and crossed half the distance to her and stopped then as though he had run against an invisible barrier.

He said, "Doc told me, Tana," and stood waiting, and Ives thought: *If she'd only smile—if she'd only say one word to him!*

But all the life seemed to go out of Tana. She placed a shoulder against the door jamb and said in a small voice, "I'll be getting back to Hammer."

Benedict said desperately, "I'd like to ride back with you."

For a moment Ives's sympathy was so strong it choked

him, but he knew that Benedict's desire could be the undoing of all of them and he said sharply, "How much prodding do you think the colonel will stand?"

Benedict looked like a man with a bullet in him who was trying to carry the weight of that lead and stay on his feet, and it took him a moment to speak. He said then, "You're right, Doc. *You*'d better be the one who takes her through the gate."

"No," Ives said. "I'll never ride through that gate again."

Benedict jerked. "I really *am* beholden!"

Ives shook his head. "I don't want you packing that notion. You were only a small part of it, Rod." He looked at Tana. "The colonel talked to me. He spoke of Texas and the trail north. He spoke of Dodge City."

Tana stood now with all the serenity shaken out of her, and she said, "Brian!" and her voice was stricken.

He said, "Nothing's changed for us, Tana," and he was remembering her hands beating against his chest, pushing him away from her. "It's just that we both know now." He looked at Elisha Lund. "You'd better be the one to take her to Hammer."

Lund had frowned his perplexity, but he asked no questions, and Ives was grateful for that. Lund said, "I'll hitch up the wagon. She can tie her horse on behind." He lifted a huge hand again; there was welcome in the gesture. "You ain't had no breakfast yet."

Ives said, "All I want to do is sleep for a million years."

He stepped down from the saddle, and one of the farmers moved forward and took the horse's trailing reins. It was Jorgensen; thus did Jorgensen acknowledge a bargain fulfilled. Ives lurched toward the shack, feeling done in; and Lund stepped aside to let him pass, and Tana lowered her eyes. When he was inside the shack, she looked at him—she'd got hold of herself again—and she said,

"Good-by, Brian," and he felt then that he would never see her again.

He said, "Good-by, Tana," and seated himself upon a chair and began tugging at his boots, being very deliberate about it, being brutal. This was how he shut her out, and it had to be like this, quick and final for both of them.

She moved out of the door and he sat holding a boot in his hand till Elisha Lund said, "Yoost climb in the bunk and snooze all you want. I'll be back soon."

Ives said, "Get her there as fast as you can. The colonel's got a right to be edgy till she shows up."

He looked about him. This shack was partitioned into two rooms and this one was the living room, he supposed, though it had a bunk built into one corner, and that made it a bedroom, too. A centering table held a huge Bible with a silver clasp and also a vase in which flowers had withered. The windows were brightly curtained; he recognized the feminine touch in flowers and curtains and remembered that Marybelle had spoken of her mother, but now he judged that Elisha Lund's wife was dead. Those withered flowers told him; there'd been no woman here these last couple of days to keep them watered.

He got off his other boot and stripped himself of his gun belt and looked for a place to hang it. A curtained doorway gave off this room; he swept the curtain aside and peered into a lean-to tacked onto the back of the shack, making a third room. Here was a small iron bed; it was darker in the lean-to, and he stepped inside and laid his gun belt upon a chair and set the boots on the floor and fell into the little bed.

He lay, his body slowly relaxing, but there was still too much tension in him for sleep to come. After a while he heard a wagon creaking in the yard; that would be Lund and Tana starting out for Hammer, he decided. He wondered about Marco Stoll; Stoll had headed this way last night, but he hadn't seen the man about and he hadn't thought to ask.

Benedict came into the shack. He said in a soft voice, "Doc?" Ives muttered, and Benedict said, "I'm getting on into town. Maw will be worried. I'll see you later, Doc. And I'll keep an eye peeled for Brule, meanwhile."

Ives muttered again, feeling too drowsy to want to make real talk. Benedict left the shack; Ives heard his boots beat against the hard-packed earth beyond the doorway until the sound diminished and was lost. He felt sorry for Benedict, remembering Benedict's reaching out toward Tana today and Tana's rearing that invisible wall between them; and his thought was that both himself and Benedict had come against such a wall, he because of Dodge City and something that had happened twenty-three years ago, Benedict because there were two breeds of men on this range and no peace between the old and the new.

Thinking this, he fell asleep.

He awoke with the strange sensation that comes to a man who has turned day into night; he awoke not realizing his whereabouts at once and wondering whether it was morning and feeling altogether topsy-turvy. Someone had pulled a chair beside the bed and was sitting there; it was Marybelle. She smiled at him in the dimness of his lean-to.

"That's my bed you've been sleeping in, Doc," she said.

She leaned over him, still smiling; it was good to find her here. She was someone circumstance had brought close to him since he'd come back to this range; her presence took the edge from his lost feeling. He reached for her, and his arms went around her and he drew her to him. Her lips came to his with no evasion; he had never imagined what her kiss would be like, but it held coolness and comfort and belied the sensual roguishness her lips had suggested. He held her thus for a long moment and then she gently removed herself from his arms. She was shaken; he could tell that; he had never known another time when she wasn't in complete command of herself.

She said, "Doc, that wasn't exactly fair."

He said, "Then I'm sorry. You came close to me just once too often."

She shook her head. "I'm the one who cheated. There's always a time when a man doesn't stand a chance. I've sat here by the bed waiting for that time."

She stood up. She laughed gaily. "You'll want something to eat. I'll get it for you."

When she was gone, he stomped into his boots. He came out into the other room and Cory Lund sat there. Ives looked at him and said, "So you came, too."

Marybelle called from the adjacent kitchen, her voice rising above the clatter of stove lids. "I couldn't hold him through the night, not without tying him. He was too sure there was big trouble in the wind."

Ives said, "Let's have a look at that arm."

Cory submitted himself to Ives's attention, and Ives unbandaged the wound and had his look and then redressed Cory's arm. Ives said, "You're coming along fine. But I meant it when I told you to take it easy. You're a hell of a patient, Cory."

Cory said grudgingly, "You're a good man at your trade, Doc."

Ives said, "The trouble lately is that I've had two trades."

Cory nodded. "Yes, I know. I told you the other day that I'd change my mind if you laid more than talk on the line. Maybe I pegged you wrong, Doc."

Ives said, "So you've talked to your father."

Cory frowned. "No, he's not back from Hammer yet. But some of the boys were still around when we rode in this morning. I know about Benedict's getting back. I know how that was worked."

Ives said, "Your dad isn't back?" He felt faint alarm. "What time of day is it?"

He stepped to the door. The sun showed mid-afternoon and the dull, droning silence of mid-afternoon lay upon Elisha Lund's yard. Chickens scratched disconsolately at the hard-packed earth; sunlight glinted from an ax in one of the chopping-blocks; a few men still loitered about the place, but not as many as had been here this morning.

Marybelle said, "Eggs are on the table."

Ives said, "I wonder what's keeping your father?"

Marybelle nodded toward a wash basin she'd filled. "You'll want to wash up."

He did this, rubbing his face on a coarse roller towel afterward and examining himself in a mirror over the kitchen washstand. Lint clung to his face; he rubbed this away with the heel of his hand. Stubble rasped against his hand; he needed a shave.

Marybelle said, "I brought your things down from Feather's place."

He sat at a table in the kitchen and Marybelle watched him eat. Cory came and stood in the doorway, saying nothing. Marybelle replenished the coffee cup and Ives emptied it and shoved it away.

"I feel like a new man," he said.

Marybelle said, "I suppose you'll be going back to Hammer."

Ives shook his head. Only now did it come to him that there was no place to go, no place but Oregon. Then he said, "I've got a ride to make if I can borrow a horse. Jensen's. I told the woman last night that I'd drop back and look at the child."

Marybelle said, "I'll ride with you."

He nodded. "I get all tangled up in fences when you're not along."

Yet he wanted to be alone. He knew this for an ungallant thought, but there was no changing it. He was suddenly rudderless; he was without aim and too empty inside to care about the small things, such as whether a man rode alone or not. He supposed he should be grateful, and he smiled at Marybelle and thanked her for the breakfast.

He got his razor out of the carpetbag and shaved. He wondered if he should wear his Prince Albert under today's sun. He decided against this, but his indecision, as he stood with the coat in his hands, was obvious.

Marybelle laughed. "Are you going to a dance or to a sickbed?"

He said, "You've got to inspire confidence. It's a trick of the trade. Don't tell anyone, will you?"

Cory said, "I'll saddle up for you," and left the shack.

The gaiety went out of Marybelle. She moved close to Ives and stood looking up at him, and she said, "What's happened to you, Doc? It's less than a day since I saw you, and meanwhile someone's hit you right between the eyes."

"It doesn't matter," he said.

"Was it that girl? Tana?"

He closed his hands and opened them. "Work is what I need," he said. "Lots of work."

Marybelle said, "I'll never set a trap for you again. Not like I did today. When you want me and some good can come out of the wanting, come to me. I'll be close by."

He reached and pinched her nose gently. He said, "Thanks, little girl."

It came to him that she was close to crying; the realization disturbed him greatly. He made himself busy checking his instrument case; he was quite thorough about this and took a great deal of time at it.

Cory shaped up in the doorway. "I've saddled for both of you."

Ives nodded. He brought his instrument case out and tied it to the saddle horn and climbed up. Marybelle mounted, too, and Ives said to Cory, "You lie low, now, remember that. You've just got to take it easy."

Cory looked to the east. "Maybe that's up to Colonel Carradine," he said.

Ives frowned. "Your dad will be here any minute. Tell him I'll be back this way this evening."

But he, too, looked to the east as he followed Marybelle who picked a way out of the yard and took a trail northward toward Jensen's place. Ives looked, but a rise of ground limited the view, and there was no telling how close Elisha Lund might be. He decided he was getting so jumpy that he was borrowing worry, and he put his mind on Jensen's place and the work for his hands. He had two trades on Sombra Range; he couldn't be a peacemaker always. The need was for the doctor now.

15

The Last Chip

THERE WAS A BLEAK ALIKENESS TO THESE HOMESTEADS, and Jensen's looked the same as the others they'd passed on their northward journeying; the tar-paper shack, the scattered outbuildings, the hard-packed yard with its scratching chickens, the garden beyond. Adversity made a familiar pattern along the upper Sombra. Ives had passed this way twice, but he might have had difficulty finding Jensen's if it hadn't been for Marybelle. She said, "Here," when the time came, and they rode into the yard and he stepped down from his horse and remembered the fear that had first come to him when Marybelle had told him about Jensen's child the other night.

"You wait outside," he ordered.

Marybelle nodded. She got down from her saddle and walked off toward the garden and began an inspection of it. Ives lifted his case from the saddle and found the shack's door open and the woman standing there. Her man was with her now; her man loomed up behind her, gaunt and red-eyed and hopeless-looking. He'd been one of those who'd gathered at Elisha Lund's place last night; he frowned at Ives.

Ives said, "I told you I'd come back."

The woman dried her hands on her apron. She was tall and rawboned and her hair kept falling into her eyes. She brushed at her forehead with the back of her hand. She was wearing a thick gold wedding ring.

"Come in," she said.

This shack was not as large as Lund's; it had only one room, and all of living was done in this room. The child's bed was in a far corner; the child lay there listlessly. He looked to be about twelve. Ives went to him and looked down and smiled and said, "Hello, young feller," trying to be brisk and professional and comforting, but there was a feeling in this shack that made him defensive; they had him pegged as belonging to Hammer.

The boy looked at him with large eyes; the boy looked scared.

Ives glanced at the parents. "Tell me about it."

Jensen moved his weight from one foot to the other, still frowning. Mrs. Jensen said, "He started getting headaches a few days ago. He just didn't have no gumption at all. He doesn't want to eat, and he doesn't sleep at night. He just tosses and turns."

Ives placed his case upon a chair and opened it. He took the boy's temperature and began a careful examination. He placed his hand on the boy's abdomen in the appendical region; he found a slight distension there. He said, "Tummy hurt?" and the boy nodded. Ives looked for rose spots on the abdomen, but there were none. He turned to the parents. "There are other children sick in this same manner?"

"Half a dozen," Jensen said. He had a deep, rumbling voice. "Beamis's is the worst, from what I've heard."

Ives snapped his case shut and picked it from the chair. "Don't go near him any more than you have to," he said. "I'll drop in again. Probably tomorrow."

Jensen said, "Ain't you going to do nothing? Ain't you

going to give him medicine? What the hell kind of doctor are you?''

It was there, the belligerency, flushed out into the open; and against it Ives put a professional aloofness. ''We have to study these things to know what they are. And we have to know what they are before we begin doctoring. He might have appendicitis. He might have something else.''

Ives went to the door; Jensen stood aside to let him pass, and Mrs. Jensen said in a small voice, ''We're obliged to you, Doctor.''

''I'll be back tomorrow,'' Ives said.

Marybelle sat upon the platform over the well, her back to the pump. Ives looked at the pump, then looked to see the location of the outhouse. He frowned. He said, ''Will you take me to Beamis's place''

Marybelle said, ''It's back down the river.''

They mounted and headed southward in silence; when Jensen's place was a piece behind them, Marybelle said, ''You look worried. Is it bad?''

''I don't know yet,'' he said.

They came to Beamis's place within the hour; here, too, was another tar-paper shack, another scattering of outbuildings, and it might have been Jensen's scrawny chickens that scratched in the yard. Beamis kept pigs; they squealed in their pen. Beamis was chopping wood; he put down his ax when the pair rode up, and he came forward slowly, another gaunt, harassed man. He said, ''You'd be the doctor,'' and he looked at Marybelle as if to find some confirmation from her that Ives's presence was professional.

Ives said, ''I've heard you have a sick child. I'd like a look at the child, if you don't mind.''

Again there was that belligerency, that feeling that he was suspect and unwanted, but this gave way to a strange gratefulness in Beamis's eyes. He said, ''Come in. Come in.''

His wife had come to the shack's door; she was slatternly and rail-thin, and worry had put years onto her. Again there was the one room, and the bed in the corner, but the patient was a girl, possibly fourteen. Fever had covered the child's lips and tongue with a dirty brown crust, and she muttered deliriously. Marybelle had followed as far as the door. Ives turned and said sharply to her, "Stay out of here!" For now he knew what he was up against, and the knowledge filled him with fear.

He looked at the parents. "How long has this been going on?"

"Two, three weeks," the woman said.

Beamis said, "When she kept getting worse, I went to town. Mr. Stoll gave me medicine." He took a bottle down from a shelf. "Here it is."

Ives pulled the cork and smelled the bottle's contents and walked to the door and flung the bottle as far out into the yard as he could. When he turned, anger had drawn his lips thin. But he said nothing. He took the child's temperature, and then he said, "Bring me a basin of cold water."

He fell to sponging the child; he worked at this an hour and more, forgetting time, forgetting everything but the need of his patient. From time to time he took the child's temperature; her delirious babbling grew less. Ives turned to the mother. "I want you to watch how I do this. I want you to be able to sponge her when I'm not around. It may have to be done often this week."

Hoofs beat out of the south and made a clatter in the yard. Through the open door Ives saw a farm boy upon an unsaddled horse, his naked heels thumping against the horse's flanks. The boy flung himself from the horse and went to Marybelle. Beamis walked out; and Ives turned back to his patient. He commenced sponging again; he kept this up for another half hour, then had a look at his thermometer. One hundred and three degrees.

Beamis had come back into the shack. Beamis paced,

saying nothing. Ives drew his sleeves across his forehead and felt like a man flung headlong into a nightmare. He said, "My God! My God!" and it was a prayer.

He remembered the parents. He said, "I'll be back again tomorrow. How many more of them are there, I wonder."

He picked up his case and came out into the yard. He saw Marybelle waiting for him; he had forgotten about Marybelle; he had forgotten about the farm boy who'd come bareback. The boy was gone.

Marybelle pulled herself slowly into her saddle. She said, "I've got to go home now. Dad's dead."

The land uptilted and Ives almost fell from his own saddle. He was thinking that there'd been much too much of everything lately. He was thinking that he'd finally go numb, but not too numb to understand this. "Hammer?" he asked and knew what the answer would be.

"The horse brought the wagon home," she said in an empty voice. "He was in it. Shot dead. That's all I know."

"You should have gone on home," he said.

"I thought you'd want to know.I knew you had your hands full in there. I told Beamis not to tell you."

"Hell!" he said. "Oh, hell!" And he rocked in his saddle.

And now there was nothing to do but ride. He had met calamity once today; he had met it again, and he was beyond thinking. They headed southward; Marybelle found her way through the maze of fences, and they said nothing to each other on that ride, but Marybelle's face was a dead woman's face. The day was about ended; the shadows marched down from the hills, and the river reflected the setting sun and ran bloody. Ives looked upon the river and shuddered.

They came to Lund's place to find the yard teeming; wagons were here, and men and women and children. More than one messenger had carried the news, Ives decided, to have caused so many to assemble so soon. Ives and Marybelle stepped from their horses in this milling crowd, and the people opened a lane for them, giving their sympathy to Marybelle by their silence; and through this lane the two moved to the shack. Elisha Lund was here; they had laid him out, as was the custom; they had placed boards upon sawhorses in the largest room, moving the table with its silver-clasped Bible aside, and Lund lay upon these boards, a blanket thrown over him, his beard rigid.

Only then did Marybelle begin weeping.

Cory Lund was in the room; he sat with his head bowed, not even looking up when the two entered. Marco Stoll was here, too; Ives remembered now that the square-type buggy had been in the yard. Stoll filled a chair and kept a respectful silence; Stoll looked properly solemn.

Ives said, "How did it happen?"

Stoll's rubbery lips moved. Stoll said, "I just got here. They tell me that the wagon came back, and Lund was in it. Some of the nesters were still here from last night; they rode out to look for sign. They found blood just beyond the fork. Lund had got that far and turned north toward Hammer. That's where he was shot, we'd guess. The tracks were pretty badly scrambled, but it looks like the wagon was turned around by a man on foot. One of Hammer's crew likely; there may have been more of them. It might have been the colonel himself. Tana seems to have gone on by horseback from there—on her own horse."

Ives said angrily, "Are these fools going to jump at that—a few tracks in the dirt?" And a fear was in him, a fear for Tana.

Stoll shrugged. "That's not for me to say." He gestured toward the laid-out body. "He's dead. That's sign enough."

The anger was still in Ives, a futile anger, a wanting to strike at something but having no tangible opponent. But from the one anger came another, and he crossed to Stoll and reached down and closed his fingers over Stoll's left wrist. Ives said, "I just came from Beamis's place. I saw the medicine you sold him. In the name of sanity, man, why don't you find out what's wrong with a patient before you start mixing a prescription?"

Stoll's little eyes glinted and he wrenched his wrist free of Ives's grasp. Stoll said, "I've tried to be friendly with you, Doc. I want to stay friendly. But keep your hands off me! I've never let any man lay a hand on me. I'm not starting now!"

Ives said, "But to be so damn careless about medicine! It's pure murder!"

Marybelle said, "Do you have to bicker here?"

Ives stepped back from Stoll. "I'm sorry," Ives said.

Cory Lund looked up. He saw Ives, but he looked through Ives without seeing him. Cory said to Marybelle, "We'll bury him tonight. Some of the neighbors are doing the digging."

Ives said, "So soon?"

Cory had that coldness in his eyes. "We've work to do, mister!"

Ives said desperately, "Let me look into this. I'll drag whoever did this to Benedict's jail, if you'll give me time. Even if it's the colonel."

"It *was* the colonel," Cory said emphatically. "No matter who pulled the trigger. He never could stand to take a beating. Any kind of beating. Dad wasn't even packing a gun. What the hell kind of a chance did Dad have?"

He was raging inside, Cory was; he was being swept an anger so great that it had no outward manifestation. There was only the coldness in his eyes. There was only the steel in his voice.

Stoll said, "You might as well know all of it, Doc. Half a dozen men got off the noon stage today. Hardcase fellows with tied-down guns. They came in from Cheyenne. They put up at the hotel, and they asked the way to Hammer."

Cory glared at Ives. "And you want to fool around trying to put a man in a jail! We've wasted too much time. We should have hit days ago when our chance was better!"

Ives looked at Marybelle, and in his look was an entreaty; he implored her support. And, looking at her, he suddenly stood alone. She had ceased her weeping; he judged that she would never weep again. She was there beside her father,and grief had torn her face apart, and shc was a stranger to Brian Ives now—no, she was more alien than that; she was an enemy. She said coldly, passionlessly, "Cory's right. I was a fool not to have seen it before."

Ives had the reckless feeling of a gambler down to his last chip, and he flung this chip out, not caring whether it brought him anything, yet caring desperately. He said, "You start leading your men toward Hammer, Cory, and I take the stage out tonight!"

"Take it and be damncd," Cory said.

"You don't understand, Cory. I'm the only doctor on this range. When I go, you're left with this fat fool who hands out any kind of medicine. You need me, but you're not going to have me if you start your war. That's a promise."

Cory said, "Then we'll get along without you."

"You can't," Ives said. "You have a typhoid fever epidemic on your hands."

Cory looked at him unbelievingly. This news was a blow to Cory; it left him stricken; it left him furious. And there the last chip lay.

16

Night of Terror

TANA HAD RIDDEN AWAY FROM ELISHA LUND'S PLACE NOT once looking back, her face wooden and her thoughts a turmoil. On the buckboard seat beside her, Lund kept his huge hands on the reins and held silent, and they climbed a rise of ground and dropped over it, Tana's saddler trailing behind. Lund reached the road to Tamerlane and wheeled along it. Tana sat staring ahead, remembering Ives tugging off his boots and dismissing her with that gesture, remembering Rod Benedict coming to help her into the buckboard and saying nothing, not even good-by, though his eyes had been eloquent enough.

She shook inwardly; she had held herself serene for so long, so very long, that she wanted now to let loose and weep.

Lund broke his silence. Lund said, "He is a goot man—a very goot man."

She supposed he was speaking of Benedict, though she couldn't be sure and she didn't ask. She wanted no sympathy; sympathy would be her complete undoing, so she made her lips stiff and looked handsome and regal and self-contained. The buckboard rattled along; the range spread before them, and she caught the distant glint of sunlight on barbed wire. Yonder lay Hammer, where cattle grazed. Lund looked in that direction; Lund's hard-planed features softened and his beard moved with his smiling.

He said, "When you are young, you want to fight against things, to change the world to your vay. It is so with my daughter. When you are older, you learn to sit back and let what is to happen happen. And one morning you wake up, and all the walls you been butting your head against have fallen down—just like the walls of Jericho."

Tana said, "Who wants to wait to be old?"

Lund shrugged. "Maybe the walls fall tomorrow. Maybe the next day. Maybe a year from now." He looked again toward Hammer. 'That is why I do not hate your grandfather. He is butting his head against a wall. Meantime, I must try to save my people from folly. Only the land stays the same. All the rest changes, whether we want it to or not."

She was strangely comforted; she looked at this man beside her and he was no longer alien, he was no longer an invader come to tear her world apart. He was wisdom and tolerance and patience; she wondered why she had never seen the philosopher behind the weathered face. He had no learning, not like Colonel Carradine's; he had no wealth. But he had learned the great fundamentals through the process of living, and thus he had amassed the greatest wealth of all. He had come to sense inevitability and to bow before inevitability and thereby defeat it. And, realizing this, Tana felt freed. What Elisha Lund had learned, she could learn likewise, and therein lay the freedom.

She said, "I never had a father to talk to."

His eyes clouded. "A man holds his children to him only so long. Then they walk their own way. Maybe, after a while, they come back."

She said, "The walls come tumbling down."

His beard twitched with his grinning. "Which one of us is supposed to be making the other feel better?"

She laughed. She said, "I'm glad I met you. So very glad."

Lund flicked the reins. "Soon now we be at Hammer."

"And you're coming into the house!" she cried. "You're going to sit with the colonel. And between you, you're going to settle this trouble for once and for all."

"That will be goot," he said solemnly.

She began talking then, a pent-up flood of talk bursting free. She told of Texas and of the migration north; she told of Marco Stoll and Jim Ives and Dave Carradine and Tom Feather. She told all of the tale the colonel had told her ten years before when she had wept because Brian Ives had left. Lund gave her his quiet attention. Then she told of Rod Benedict, who had come to work for Hammer, and she confessed to moonlight rides the colonel hadn't known about; she confessed to stolen kisses. She talked freely; she had talked to no man in this fashion, and the talking was good.

Afterward Lund said, "All the time you have looked backward, never forward. And you have been too much alone. That was not goot."

He lifted his eyes. "Look. Here is the fork in the road!"

They turned northward toward Hammer; they rode in silence again, but it was a different kind of silence; it was a communion. Tana felt warm inside; she felt fetterless. They came into the shadow of one of the many cutbanks flanking this road, and the shadow was cool and comforting—until the gun spoke. The sound broke the silence sharply, and Elisha Lund sagged gently against Tana, blood on him; Lund died against Tana.

But for a moment there was still strength in him. He used to it haul at the reins, but perhaps that was some reflex beyond his bidding. His shoulder was against Tana's, and in this stunned moment she knew no fear nor even surprise; she'd been swept beyond those things. She got an arm around him; his eyes were already glazing, but in his last lucidity he could still measure and weigh, and he knew what had happened and what it could portend; she could read that knowledge in his eyes.

He said thickly, "It's lost now—everything—"

She knew what he meant, and she knew that even now he was selfless, concerned with how many men might die because he was dying, and she said, "No!" frantically. "I won't let it happen!"

Then he was dead.

Brule came sliding down the cutbank, gun in his hand and his face wolfish, with his yellowed teeth showing. Tana knew him; she had seen him a time or two in Tamerlane and had heard him called by name, and she had listened to Ives's feverish blabbling of his encounter with this same man. Brule had worked himself up to the killing pitch; moreover, fear was in him, and that was what made him really dangerous. He came to the buckboard and yanked at Tana's arm.

"Down, you!" he ordered.

He dragged her from the buckboard and, keeping a hold on her elbow, fetched her with him as he went about unfastening her horse from behind the vehicle. Lund's team was smelling blood and showing skittishness. Brule released Tana and grasped at the reins and brought team and buckboard around, facing them south. He slapped them hard with the reins and let them clatter away. Tana found her legs and turned to run; Brule pounced upon her. His hands were offensive; he got her to her horse and made her mount and produced pigging strings from his pocket and proceeded to lash her hands to the saddle horn.

Tana said stonily, "Hammer will kill you for this!"

He looked to the north, the whites of his eyes showing, and she sensed the nature of his fear. Hammer's gate wasn't so far away, and the sound of the shot might have carried. He cursed her obscenely, then led her horse around the cutbank. On its far side, hidden from the road, his own mount stood with trailing reins. He climbed carefully into the saddle—he was still favoring his right leg—and began leading Tana's horse away from the road.

She could have shouted, but there was no one to hear. She let herself be led along, keeping her eyes on Brule's wide shoulders, but now the shock was leaving her and sickness came, and she was afraid she would faint. She was remembering Elisha Lund dead; his blood was on her blouse. She was remembering his body bouncing in the buckboard as the team had galloped south. She forced this picture out of her mind.

She wondered at Brule's intent as concerned her; she had expected to die with Lund, but now she supposed she was to be held for ransom. This Brule, as far as she knew, was a lone wolf, a drifter, and she presumed this to be some game of his own. But she recalled how methodically he had turned Lund's team around and headed the buckboard homeward; she recalled that Brule had lain in wait for Brian Ives another day, and she wondered then what real pattern lay behind this procedure. Her head ached and her mouth was dry, and she couldn't fight off fear.

At first it seemed that Brule moved aimlessly across the prairie, and then Tana again saw sunlight glinting on barbed wire, and shortly they were paralleling Hammer's fence northward yet keeping a good distance away. They rode steadily for an hour and another; the Sombra Hills drew nearer, and Tana realized that the hills were their destination. And now she saw Brule's strategy; he was keeping between Hammer and the strung-out nester places; he was running this narrow gauntlet boldly, and though help lay to the right and the left, Tana felt as remote as if they were on the moon.

Twice Brule stopped, his head tilted, his whole body listening. On these occasions he said, "You keep quiet," saying it ominously. Neither time did she hear anything; whatever had disturbed him escaped her notice, but she prayed then, prayed hard.

Soon they were climbing into the area of stunted trees. She could look back and see the Sombra and the smoke rising from ranch house and nester shack, and Tamerlane shimmering distantly. Brule moved with greater surety; she sensed that he was near his destination, and her fear grew. She closed her eyes for long minutes, trying to detach herself from reality, but always when she opened her eyes the first thing she saw was Brule's broad back.

Into deeper timber, Brule searched out a game trail and followed along it, but there was a regular maze of these trails and at many forks he hesitated. Then, suddenly Tana knew where he was headed, and relief left her teetering in the saddle, Feather's place! He was taking her to Feather's place, and Marybelle and Cory Lund were there, but Brule didn't know that! At first this seemed unbelievable luck, until she put herself in Brule's place and did his kind of thinking. South, east, and west were closed to him, for Tamerlane, Hammer, or the nester settlement held dangers. Therefore he'd had to turn north, and the only shelter in this section was Feather's shack.

She tried not to let her face show elation. Brule had found the right trail and they moved along in single file; soon they were in the clearing before the shack. Brule dismounted carefully; his gun came into his hand again, and he said once more, "You keep quite." He made no attempt to gag her, and she wondered how he could be so sure that she was intimidated—until she looked down and saw Elisha Lund's blood.

He moved slowly across the clearing, leading her horse and his; a vast silence held all the hills, and the heart went out of Tana then, for now she sensed that the place was deserted. Between suns the Lunds had left. Brule reached the door; it was partially open, and he kicked at it. He peered inside; he grinned. Then he moved to Tana and fumbled at the knots holding her wrists.

He said, "Git down."

She almost fell. He caught at her, steadying her. Again the feel of his fingers revolted her. She wrenched free; he seized her and shoved her inside the shack.

Tom Feather was sleeping in the bunk.

Now Tana glimpsed a new shadow of hope, but Feather rolled over and propped himself up on an elbow and brushed away his tangled mane with a sweep of his hand. He said, "Howdy." Feather was surprised, but he showed no real curiosity, no real interest. He was in that peculiar detached state of mind in which Ives had found him at the creek bank yesterday; he had these moments when he knew nobody.

Tana said, "It's me—Tana!"

Feather frowned. He seemed to be wrestling with something beyond his comprehension. Finally he said, "Make yourself at home."

Brule said, "Yes, make yourself at home. We'll be here a couple of days."

Tana let herself down into a chair; it was sit down or fall down. Brule took a chair and spun it around and sat straddling it, folding his arms on top of the chair back. He sat like this for a long time, watching the two of them. Feather climbed out of the bunk and yawned and stretched himself. He was fully clothed, even to his boots. He made no overt move, and some of the tension went out of Brule.

"Couple horses outside," Brule said. "Put 'em away, if you've got a place for 'em. But leave 'em saddled."

Tana thought: *He's fixing it so he can get away fast.*

Feather said, "There's a lean-to out back."

Feather left the shack; Brule kept his unblinking gaze upon Tana. Once he rubbed his hand across the stubble on his chin.

Tana said, "Would you mind telling me why you dragged me here?"

"You won't be hurt none," Brule said. "Not if you behave yourself. You're just staying here a couple of days." And he shook with inward laughter.

She tried making sense out of this; she wondered again if it was ransom he wanted. She knew what would happen when she didn't show back at Hammer; she knew what the colonel would think. There was more at stake here than Brule understood—or was she wrong about that? Perhaps he was hiding her out in order to foment trouble. She wondered if she should accuse him of that; she decided against doing so.

Feather came back into the shack. It was getting on to dusk, and Feather poked into the stove and laid a fire. Before food was on the table, it was lamp-lighting time. Feather got one of the lamps burning and set it in the center of the table. The three ate silently; Tana had no appetite. Feather gathered up the plates afterward.

"A lot of strange faces in the hills these days," he said.

Brule looked at Tana. "What's the matter with him?"

Tana said softly, "Can't you tell? He's sick in the head."

Feather climbed into the bunk. He lay there, his hands locked behind his head, his eyes gazing at the ceiling; he was alone with himself again. Brule grew bored; Brule roamed the shack aimlessly and looked often from the door. Then he straddled a chair again and sat in silence, the minutes running on. There was no sound but the sputtering of the lamp, and then Tana slowly came to realize that something was in this shack that hadn't been here before. At first she was only mildly disturbed; she had grown tired of the steadiness of Brule's gaze, and she had kept her eyes away from him. Now she looked and read his face, and her fear rose and choked her. His face was wooden, but he was breathing hard, and his eyes betrayed him. She sensed that his desire had been no part of his intent when he'd first brought her here, but that made her terror no less.

Brule saw her glance and was done with pretense. Brule looked toward Feather. "Old-timer, go take a walk for yourself," Brule said.

Feather said drowsily, "Eh?"

"Get out of here!" Brule said savagely.

Feather swung his legs to the floor and came to a stand, looking from one to the other in bewilderment.

Tana cried, "No, Tom!" and freed herself of her numbness and ran toward the door. Brule spilled his chair getting off it; he snatched at her and flung her hard against the wall. He began cursing her.

Tana screamed, "Tom!"

Feather's face pucked with anger. "You keep your hands off her!" he shouted.

Brule dragged out his gun and waved it; and Tana, pressed against the wall, gave up hope. Guns were the terror of Tom Feather's existence; she had seen him cringe at the sight of one bracketed to a wall, and she knew how he had come by his phobia. She expected Feather to wilt before the threat of Brule's gun and go scurrying into the darkness, but Feather had found some strange reservoir of courage. Feather charged at Brule, and this was suicidal, but it was also magnificent. It was as though a man who had dealt in futility a score of years had now shed himself of futility and found a cause. And so Tom Feather died.

The roar of the gun in the confines of the shack was

like thunder in a well. Feather spun about, his hands clutching his chest; he went down to his knees and bowed forward, looking strangely devout. He shook his wild mane; his eyes lifted to the window of the shack, and he screamed, "Stoll! Marco Stoll!" Then he fell forward.

Brule glared about. Brule looked toward the window and ran outside; and Tana made another lunge for the door then, but her legs wouldn't hold her. She stumbled; she tried picking herself up; she became aware of clattering hoofs, of some great commotion outside. And then, astonishingly, the colonel was in the doorway. The colonel's scar flamed, and the man cried, "In the name of God, what is this?"

"Brule—" Tana said weakly.

"He just rode away," the colonel said. "He must have heard me coming up."

"Stoll—outside—window—" Tana muttered.

Carradine went through the door as though released from a bow. He came back in a few minutes; he shook his head. "Nobody is out there," he said. "I even lighted matches. Not a sign of a footprint beneath the window."

Tana had got to her feet; she reeled, and the colonel moved to support her. Tana had never seen him so shaken. He said, incoherently, but with a strange intentness, as though the explanation was important, "I came up here to examine the lie of the land. I thought perhaps I might post some of the crew at the shack later. This is the back door to Hammer. Somebody might think of that when the shooting starts."

"Shooting?" She looked at Tom Feather upon the floor and shuddered. Then she understood what the colonel was implying. "Lund was fetching me home," she cried. "They kept their bargain. Brule waylaid us and shot Lund and brought me here. Don't you understand it? It just *looked* as if they were still holding me!"

Carradine said darkly, "I only know you didn't come back. I was going to give them until morning. Onc of thc reasons I took this ride was to keep from going insane. I've men coming from Cheyenne. Perhaps they're already waiting at Hammer. I'll put an end to all this business!"

She remembered Elisha Lund dying; she remembered her pledge to Lund, and she tore herself away from the colonel. "*No!*" she said, and this was her first real defiance of him.

17

Ives Walks with Death

NOW IVES BEGAN HIS WALK WITH DEATH.

First there was the funeral of Elisha Lund; they buried him on a slight bluff overlooking the Sombra, overlooking the nester settlement; they buried him at dusk of the day he'd died; Cory was single-minded about that. Cory was a shaken man; he had talked to Beamis and Jensen and some of the others, and Ives judged that he'd mentioned the ultimatum Ives had laid down. There had been much shaking of heads; there had been many glances directed Ives's way; there had been some sawing of the air with hands. But Ives had allies; he knew it now. Allies of the moment. Those with sick children no longer cared about Hammer; the need at home was their great need.

Elisha Lund had been placed in a crude coffin which someone had hastily fashioned. They carried this coffin to its hole at sunset; they stood grouped around the hole, men in denim and women in calico and children turned quiet by the soberness of the moment. One among them took upon himself the job of delivering a sermon; he was another gaunt man, and he had a nasal twang to his speech.

He knew his Scripture and he chose many texts, sprinkling them at random through his talk. He kept to no straight path in his sermon; he wandered through wordy mazes.

Ives looked down at Elisha Lund before the lid was fastened. Ives remembered that night in Tamerlane's jail when Lund had come to him and Ives had expected wrath but Lund had fetched him tolerance instead. Ives thought that here lay a friend, and he thought, too, that the rag-tag preacher might have done better to have taken his text from Shakespeare: *If you have tears, prepare to shed them now—*

Marco Stoll was present, as were several other townsmen, and, oddest of odd, a couple of cattlemen from across the Sombra. Stoll still had a look of professional sympathy upon his face; there was no reading Stoll. But a real grief rode the homesteaders; they had lost a leader.

The preacher ended a windy prayer; hands busied themselves at the lowering of the box. Ives remembered Marybelle's saying that any man should own at least as much earth as he needed to be buried in. He looked at Marybelle across the grave. She had the face of a sleepwalker. He looked at her, but he thought of Tana; he was worried about what had really happened on the road to Hammer today. Whichever way his thoughts ran, they snarled themselves in worry. If Hammer had done for Elisha Lund and packed Tana off to the ranch, therein lay the makings of disaster. But supposing it hadn't been Hammer—He tried not to think about that.

The funeral was over. The dirt was falling and the crowd began to disperse, and Cory clapped on his narrow-brimmed sombrero and took Marybelle by the elbow. She let him lead her away. The crowd spilled down into Lund's yard and milled aimlessly; they'd showed no guns at the service, but the guns were with them, in the wagons, in the buggies. The cattlemen from across the Sombra stepped up into saddles and headed for the ford. Stoll wheeled his buggy out of Lund's yard and took the road to Tamerlane. Ives stood in the yard, not wanting to go inside Lund's shack. There would be food heaped about, brought by neighbors for a brother and sister who didn't want to eat; there would be prairie flowers and no eyes to see them. There would be grief.

Someone plucked at Ives's sleeve. He found a bearded man, harassed by worry. He had seen this man before; suddenly he recalled that the man had been one of the two who'd backed Cory against him that first day in Tamerlane. The man said, "You're a doctor?"

Ives knew what was coming. Ives said, "Yes."

"My oldest boy—"

"I'll go along home with you," Ives said.

And now indeed did he begin his walk with death.

He was not to sleep that night. No other disease demanded so much from a doctor as typhoid, and the case he rode to attend was in the dread third-week stage and there seemed to be a bad heart condition as well. Ives sat by the bed through the dark hours, feeling lost, feeling impotent. His patient was emaciated and had a pulse so feeble that time and again Ives was sure it had flickered out. But the boy was alive when morning came, and Ives pulled himself wearily into a saddle and promised the people he'd be back. Now it was another day, and there were the patients he'd attended the day before, the patients he'd promised to look in on again.

Jensen's boy was better; so was Beamis's girl. But there were new cases demanding attention. Ives got so that he left no bedside without expecting to find some frantic messenger awaiting him.

Somewhere in that day's traveling, Marybelle found him. He was sponging a feverish patient, trying desperately to reduce the fever. He was wishing he had a trained nurse.

He came upon Marybelle in the yard when the work was done. She still wore the face of a stranger, and her voice was wooden. Marybelle said, "She's safe."

At first he didn't grasp her meaning; he thought she was speaking of one of his patients. His face must have showed his bewilderment.

Marybelle said, "Cory's making no move against Hammer. You've got him in a split stick, and he knows it. But he did some scouting. With field glasses. Tana's on Hammer. He got a glimpse of her."

Ives said, "Thanks." For a moment he felt less worry.

Marybelle nodded towards the shack he'd just quitted. "How is it?"

"Stay out of there!" he said sharply.

She made a futile gesture with her hands. "Is there nothing can be done to stop it?"

He shrugged. "Some Britisher is supposed to have developed an anti-typhoid inoculation. I remember reading about it in a medical journal a while back. But such things take time to get into general use. That hope is for another year."

His glance dwelt on her; he wanted to ask her to help him, but he wanted, even more, to have her volunteer to help. He could drag no one through the shadows in which he walked. But she was still an alien; she was still standing aloof from him; she had buried part of herself with Elisha Lund.

She must have felt his glance; her face softened just a little. "When you need a place to sleep or something to eat, come to us," she said.

"Thanks," he said and helped her into her saddle.

He stood numbly in this yard, watching her ride away, wanting to call after her and yet not wanting to. He had to stop and think where he must go next. He pulled himself aboard the borrowed horse that had belonged to Elisha Lund.

Shack after shack—gaunt, harassed faces high-planed by flickering lamplight—the dawn edging around the drawn blinds—feet pacing restlessly upon uncarpeted planking—the sobbing of mothers—fever and delirium and the futile fight. No two cases exactly alike, and the treatment varying with the symptoms. Endless sponging, and sometimes a farmer dispatched hastily to Tamerlane with a carefully written list of medicines to be fetched from Stoll's drugstore. Food snatched quickly when there was time for eating. More than once Ives found himself dozing in his saddle. He slept at Lund's one night. Cory was there; Cory treated him with a frigid politeness.

And always there was the other menace and the reminder of it. Nester men let their work go undone; weeds thrived, and sometimes work stock waited for feed and water. Nester men went armed, and there were meetings and alarms in the night, but they kept the peace.

The man who had built a coffin for Elisha Lund had more work to do; Ives lost two patients in a single night, and there were two funerals. The next day there was a third. Death had suddenly become commonplace; death roosted on every man's doorstep. And Ives forgot what it was to sleep.

He came to Cory one day. He talked to Cory, not caring much how Cory took it. He said, "I think I know what's causing this thing. The water. These farmers have been using wells instead of hauling from the river. You've got men standing around with guns in their fists, doing nothing. Put them to loading barrels into wagons and hauling water from the Sombra. I want that water boiled. And I want every well in the settlement filled in or boarded over."

Cory nodded. "I'll have it done," he said. He laughed,

and his laughter had an edge of hysteria. "Have you heard? We don't need to watch so close. Those Cheyenne gunmen never got to Hammer."

Ives had forgotten about the gunmen.

"They heard there was an epidemic on this range," Cory said. "They lit out."

Ives shook his head. There was probably some sort of poetic justice in a little good coming out of a great deal of bad, but he was too tired to think about it. He said, "Typhoid's a disease that hits people in adolescence or early adult life. Anybody over thirty-five is fairly safe. And some people are quite immune to it."

Cory said, "They weren't taking any chances. They'd have bucked bullets, but they wouldn't buck typhoid."

Ives went on about his business. He felt that he'd found the means of stopping the epidemic from spreading farther, but he had at least a dozen patients now, and his days and nights had become an endless routine. He was winning these nester people to him; no longer did they treat him merely as an instrument for which they had a need; sometimes they smiled at him now, sometimes they made friendly talk. But he was too wrapped up in his work to care about this personal victory; he was pitted against the black angel, and he wrestled mightily with his adversary.

Cory kept his word. Cory had water hauled from the Sombra, and men bent their backs over shovels and the wells were filled in. Ives saw crews at work as he rode from one homestead to another. But still there were fresh cases; the sick, from whom the germ discharged, were isolated as much as possible, but the shacks were small and sometimes a parent came down with the disease. There was no stopping it; it was like a fire running wild.

"You dug your wells so they'd be handy to the house," Ives told one nester. "Then you put your outhouses on a rise of ground away from the house. Every last one of you made the same mistake; you never thought about seepage. That's why you've got polluted wells."

Again he went to Cory. He found Cory directing the work of a shovel crew, and every man of them had a gun belted about his waist, and Ives knew that only half of them were at work. The others were patrolling the fringe of the settlement, keeping an eye alert for an attack from Hammer. Ives called Cory aside.

"What we need is a hospital," Ives said.

Cory sleeved sweat from his face; he had been doing some of the work in spite of his sore arm. He had matured immeasurably these past days; one day, Ives judged, he would look like his father. Cory said, "A hospital?"

"A shack will do. One big enough to put all the sick in it together. Then we won't have them handing the fever to others. And I'll have them all where I can work on them. They won't be dying on me while I'm riding from one place to another."

Cory nodded. "We'll get to work on it."

Ives measured this youngster. Ives thought: *You're obeying me because it's best for your people. But you're remembering that I've got you hog-tied, and you're hating me for it.*

He nudged his horse. "I've got to be getting along."

And so he went his endless rounds. Now the faces were beginning to blur. He would be in Jensen's shack, working on the boy, and he would need a hand with the eternal sponging, and Mrs. Beamis would clumsily take over. He would be surprised to find her here until he would remember the ride he'd made from one place to the other, and then he'd wonder how much sleeping he'd done in the saddle.

There were more funerals. It got so that he could be sitting at a bedside and look out through a window and see a group of people trailing by, a small coffin perched upon the shoulders of four of the men, the weeping women stumbling after them, the self-appointed preacher trailing the lot. The settlement had been too new to have a cemetery; it had one now.

And so death smiled.

He learned to know the many signs to dread them. Exhaustion for a patient in the second or third week, sometimes a sudden sinking if the heart was bad. Hemorrhage from the intestines. Perforation of an intestinal ulcer—sudden, intense abdominal pains, vomiting, rapid, flickering pulse, cold, clammy skin, an ominous fall of temperature. These things marked the end. And then there would be a call to another shack and a child or a parent with headaches and lassitude and discomfort, sleepless and feverish at night, the temperature rising step by step the first week until the highest point was reached. A new case for the doctor.

Ives lost track of time. He didn't know whether it was a week or a month since Elisha Lund had been buried. He didn't know what it was to get out of all of his clothes, and he had forgot to shave for many days. He had grown sparer; he seemed taller, and the stoop to his shoulders was more pronounced. He saw the shack going up that was to be the hospital, and he was aware of its getting nearer to completion and therefore he was aware of time passing. But there was no meaning to time.

On this one day he sat by the bedside of a new patient, busy at his sponging and trying the while to comfort a mother who had been reduced to weeping incoherency. His words were a drone in his own ears; his hands made mechanical movements; he was a man who had become an automaton. He heard a horse come into the yard; he supposed it bore some frantic messenger demanding his presence elsewhere. He didn't even look up when the rider stood in the doorway, a shadow falling across him.

She said, "Brian—"

It was her voice that reached into him and brought him around. Tana stood there wearing the divided riding skirt and sombrero she'd worn when last he'd seen her. Only the blouse was different. He didn't know that she would never wear that blouse again, that it had had Elisha Lund's blood on it.

She said, "We heard about the sickness here. I've come to help you, if I can."

He was too stunned to truly hear her, but he was aware of her presence, tensely aware of it. He wanted to shout at her, to tell her to get out of here, that death lurked in this place. She took a step forward.

"There must be something I can do," she said.

"Yes," he said. "You can help me with this sponging. Come here; I'll show you how."

He knew he was wrong; he knew he should be sending her on her way. But he was too tired; he needed help too desperately. He looked at her; he saw the sincerity in her face. In him then was a need for weeping and a feeling that he should be down upon his knees.

18

The Road to Tamerlane

HE DIDN'T TAKE TIME TO INQUIRE INTO THE MIRACLE THAT had brought Tana to him, or even to think about it. Not at first. She was someone to lean upon, and he was deeply grateful, too grateful to care about the whys and the wherefores. He took her with him on his rounds that first day; once again a horse wearing Hammer's brand stood in nester yards, but the people, too, had grown apathetic; the people accepted Tana as incuriously as Ives had accepted her.

They met Cory on their riding. Cory touched his hat brim at sight of Tana and went on about his business; later Ives was to learn that Tana had come first that day to the Lund place and had been directed to Ives by Cory. There had been brief talk between Cory and Tana, and good had come of it.

From bedside to bedside Ives took Tana, and his was the job of turning her into a trained nurse in a single day. He told her much about typhoid; he described its various stages and the signs that indicated these stages, and he put her to taking temperatures and to sponging. He watched her work, and he remembered the day he had come back to Hammer, feverish from Brule's bullet and how she had cared for him then, her every movement precise. He smiled, knowing now that he might go and sleep.

He was able to revise his work schedule in the days that followed. He could send Tana to attend to some of the milder cases; she reported symptoms and progress to him, sparing him needless trips. He was even able to spend some time supervising the building of the hospital shack. Moreover, he was able to rest, and he took to shaving again. There was another death the first week Tana assisted him, but several bad cases had been pulled over the hump, and he felt at last that victory might be in sight, the long struggling nearly done.

But still nester men wore guns; still they looked toward Hammer.

One day Rod Benedict came to the nester settlement seeking Ives. Ives and Tana were working together that day, and Benedict waited outside a shack for them; and when Ives came to climb into the saddle, Benedict said, "Howdy, Doc." Ives shook hands with him. Benedict said, "Just dropped by to let you know I've been trying to cut sign on Brule. The ground's opened and swallowed him."

Tana came out; Tana heard the last of this. She shuddered. Benedict gravely removed his sombrero. He looked at Tana, smiling with his lips, his eyes hungry, and then he said, "Mind if I tag along awhile? I've got nothing special to do."

The three made the rounds together; there was little talk among them; they kept stirrup to stirrup whenever they could, Tana in the middle; and Benedict was quick to open the gates. Thus they spent the hours of an afternoon, but always there were the shacks where they stopped, and always Benedict had to wait in the yard then, and thus was he shut out. They were working southward, and at suppertime, when Tana and Ives were invited to stop over at the shack they were visiting, Benedict pulled himself into his saddle.

"I'll be getting along," he said.

It came to Ives that Benedict looked graver, maturer; there was only the ghost of his boyishness in him. They had all been seasoned, Ives judged; the shadow that lay upon the Sombra had had its effects everywhere. He wondered about the colonel; he wondered what change had come to Hammer.

Benedict said, "I'm batching now. Maw took the stage out a couple of nights ago. Heading for Kansas. Said she was afraid of the sickness that's going around. I don't think she ever liked it this far west."

His glance touched Tana; he looked lost. Tana's smile reached across to him; her smile was wistful, but it promised nothing.

"So long," Benedict said.

The nester woman appeared in the doorway of the shack. "Supper's ready," she called.

That night Ives slept at Lund's, leaving Tana with one of the patients. And so the endless rounds continued, but the hospital shack was finished sooner than Ives expected. Then came the moving of the patients to it; they came in wagons and upon improvised stretchers, and Ives fetched the last one in his arms. The hospital consisted of one big room with two rows of beds neatly spaced; Ives stood in the doorway and regarded it and felt humble and proud and terribly tired.

Cory was here. Cory waved his hand and said, "How does it suit you, Doc?"

Ives said, "Just fine," and his look met Cory's, and then they were friends.

Cory said, "We all got to jumping at shadows for a

while, Doc. Tana told me, the day she came here. It was Brule who did for Dad and packed her off. We could have made a bad mistake that day.'' Cory made a fist of his right hand. ''I've been looking for Brule. He must have skipped the country.''

''Brule?'' Ives said speculatively and tried to follow his thoughts through, but a patient in one of the beds was babbling deliriously; he had still to be the doctor.

Tana came to him. Tana looked tired. She brushed a lock of black hair from her forehead, and she seemed to reel. She said, ''I'm going to Hammer for a day or two.''

He wanted to say that he still needed her, but he had no right to say it. She had given of herself unstintingly; he fumbled for words of gratitude.

Tana said, ''*She*'ll be giving you a hand until I can get back. She's worked with me several times lately.''

He looked and saw Marybelle at the bedside of a patient. He shouldered among the milling parents and walked to where Marybelle worked. Marybelle glanced up at him, some of her old roguishness in her face. Marybelle said, ''Yes, Doc. I know when I've had coals of fire heaped on my head.''

He said, ''I learned from her myself.''

He turned back to Tana. Tana was gone; so was Cory Lund. Ives asked a question. Cory was escorting Tana to Hammer's gate.

Now Ives's work was easier for him. He had a bed for himself here in the hospital, and he could make his rounds without leaving this building. He had stopped the spread of the infection by checking it at its source; all drinking-water came from the Sombra now and was boiled as an extra precaution; and the patients were isolated here in the hospital. He still had nights when he sat through the darkness till sunrise; he still had nights of impotency when no skill was of any avail. But one by one the beds began emptying; one by one the patients were going home. There was a last funcral, a last weeping; the plague was beaten.

He found a day when he could leave Marybelle with the patients, and on this day he strode about aimlessly, a wooden-minded man who had walked too long with death. He came to the Sombra; he found a grassy place along the bank and seated himself and looked across the waters and dreamed without dreaming. And here Tana found him.

He was too lost in tiredness to hear her coming. When she sat down beside him, he lifted his eyes and saw her horse among the willows. She looked drawn, but she was more handsome than ever. She plucked a blade of grass and put it between her teeth, then let her hands lie in her lap. She sat for a long time, saying nothing, and then she said, "Hammer is no more, Brian."

He stirred. He said, "What's that?"

"The colonel's leaving. On tonight's stage."

It left him stunned; it left him groping for words.

"He's divided up Hammer among the hands, giving them each the ground they originally homesteaded for him. Some will be staying; some will be drifting on. It will be farm country soon, I imagine."

A picture came to him; he saw the fences encroaching upon Hammer, crisscrossing the acres, and wheat nodding at the sun, a sea of wheat. He saw inevitability and bowed to it, but he felt an infinite sadness. "And the colonel?" he asked.

"Going back to Texas. Part of him never left there."

He stared out across the waters, not fully grasping this, yet understanding numbly that all the trouble was ended; there would be no fight now. Then he said, "Why?"

She said, "His decision was made from many things. First, there were those gunmen deserting him because of the epidemic. He was crippled before he could start fighting. Then there was the typhoid itself. That swung the balance the other way, but it swung it too far. How could he hit at a people who were already stricken? The odds had to be somewhere near even for the colonel, one way or the other."

He said, "There was more to it than that!"

She met his gaze. She said, "Elisha Lund died knowing that all hell was apt to be let loose. Before he died, I promised him that I'd take up where he left off. The night the colonel took me away from Brule, there was a showdown. I told the colonel that the day he made war against the nesters would be the day I'd ride away from Hammer forever. That licked him, I think. Then, when we heard of the plague, I came to help you. When I went back to Hammer, he'd made his plans. Now he's headed for Tamerlane to take the stage."

He heard her out, turning over in his mind the things she said; and it seemed incredible that he had come home to pit himself against the colonel only to have the colonel's opposition dissolve. Yet it had not been so simple as this; he knew that. He remembered the colonel's crumbling when Carradine had learned that Tana was hostage to the nesters for Benedict's return; he had glimpsed the colonel's Achilles' heel that dawn and not realized it.

His glance touched Tana. "And you?"

"Hammer's house is mine. I'll stay there. I'll run a few cattle till I decide to sell and move on."

He said quietly, "You broke the back of this thing."

She said, "I'd have made my bid too late. You held the trouble off just long enough, Brian."

He said, "Then we did it together."

Again he pictured Hammer partitioned, and again he was saddened. It was the closing out of an old day; it meant peace along the Sombra, but he was saddened. Not yet was Elisha Lund's wisdom his; not yet could he fully adjust himself to what had had to be. There was that much of cattledom in the core of him.

He said, "What of Tom Feather?"

She said, "Didn't you know? Tom's dead." And she told him the story of her abduction then, all of it.

First he felt a terrible anger against Brule, but that was tempered by the thought of Feather's sacrifice, of Feather's final courage. "Perhaps dying was the best for Tom," he said, not meaning to sound shallow. "He would have been helpless without Hammer."

"Poor Tom," she said. "As he was dying, he pointed at the window and shouted Marco Stoll's name—as though Stoll were out there. But when the colonel looked, there were no tracks beneath the window."

Ives harked back to that night; it seemed an eternity ago. "That was the night Lund was buried," he recalled. "Stoll was here, at the funeral. I saw him. Tom was just having another of his delusions."

She said, "He was so afraid of guns. You know why. Yet he was so brave at the end."

He turned this over in his mind; his thoughts were sluggish, his thoughts were like footsteps in mud. He'd had no time for thinking of anything lately but the needs of the nester people. But now his mind touched upon many things he had learned since his return to the Sombra; he subconsciously fitted these shreds of knowledge together and suddenly he had created a recognizable whole, for to these he had added Feather's dying words. And so a truth stood revealed.

He came to his feet so abruptly as to startle Tana. He stood staring, his hands clenching and unclenching. He said, "My God! The colonel's a dead man!"

She didn't understand him, of course. She looked puzzled; she pulled herself to a stand.

"What is it, Brian?" she asked.

Ives said, "He left him alive all these years because he wanted to deal him worse than death. That was his scheme; I can see it now. A war with the nesters was to have ruined the colonel. But the colonel's given up the fight; he's going back to Texas. Don't you suppose that news has got around? And now there's nothing left for him to do but kill the colonel!"

"Him? Who, Brian?"

"Stoll! Marco Stoll!"

She looked puzzled. "I don't understand. Stoll's never shown an enmity toward the colonel."

He seized her arm. "Give me your horse," he said. "It's faster than any nester horse." He didn't wait for her permission; he ran to the mount and flung himself into the saddle and headed through the willows, bending low and keeping an arm before his face, riding recklessly.

Now the tiredness was gone out of him; there was no time for tiredness, not with this desperate urgency sinking its spurs into him. He roared through a nester yard; chickens squawked wildly, fluttering out of his way; he headed for the road the nesters took to town. He made a mental map of the terrain, and he realized that the road was the long way. The crow flew a shorter route to Tamerlane. But he was afraid to head overland; there would be gopher holes in the prairie, and there might be fences; he could risk no disaster, no delay. He took to the road and stayed with it. He asked everything of the horse.

A mile along the road, he remembered that he carried no gun. He'd quit wearing his gun since the plague had kept him busy; he'd left holster and belt at Lund's place. He didn't turn back. He could get a gun in Tamerlane.

He wondered how Carradine was traveling; he'd forgot to ask Tana. He supposed that Carradine had taken a saddle horse from Hammer, planning to leave the mount at the livery stable. He reached the fork in the road and looked for sign, not wasting much time at this. There was too much sign; it was meaningless. He roared southward, following the twists and turns of the road, stopping only to blow the horse when he had to, begrudging every minute spent this way. He came to the shadow of the cutbank where Brule had waited for him that first day, and he gave a thought to danger. He knew Brule now for what the man was, a hired hand; he knew who was behind Brule.

He saw the Sombra glinting in the sun; the road had veered near the river again. Yonder was the place where he'd first met Marybelle. He'd ridden this road in Stoll's buggy. Irony beyond irony!

Tana's horse began heaving beneath him, but still he kept to a killing pace; from a rise of land he glimpsed Tamerlane, and he was heartened. Yet a steady fear beat through him; he might be too late.

The shadows were growing long; the day was nearly done. The horse faltered; the horse almost went down. From another rise Ives saw Tamerlane again; he was close to town. All the road ahead was within his range of vision, but the road was naked. He begged the horse for speed, babbling crazily. He came roaring across the last of the distance; he came into the street of Tamerlane and saw the stage pulled before the depot, and relief strangled him as he flung out of the saddle.

The stage driver was loading baggage; the stage was empty.

"Colonel Carradine?"

The driver spat into the dust. "Yeah, he bought hisself a ticket. Asked me when I'd be pulling out and took his saddler to the livery."

This much of Ives's judgment had been correct. He started up the street afoot, and he saw the colonel emerge from the livery stable and come walking toward him. The colonel was dressed as always in staid black; the colonel looked imperiously Old South and self-contained. The colonel was saying farewell to a good share of his life, but he was giving Tamerlane no last lingering glance as he paced the planking.

Lamps were just winking to life; the street was almost deserted at this hour. Ives ran toward the colonel; he tried to shout, but the sound he forced out seemed a feeble croak. Still, it stopped the colonel. It stopped the colonel in the precise spot where Ives had once stood and been accosted by Cory Lund—the spot across the street from the drugstore.

Ives thought: *The fool! The fool!*

The colonel was staring at him as though Ives were mad. The colonel's aristocratic face was a question mark. But up there in the darkened window of Stoll's quarters something moved slightly, and it was all the sign Ives needed.

This was no time for talk, not with the seconds running out. Ives sprinted forward and dived at the colonel; his shoulder struck against the colonel's knees, and the two of them went down in a tangle.

That was when the shotgun boomed.

19

The Sound of Guns

THERE WAS THIS TO BE SAID FOR THE COLONEL; HE WAS a good man in a pinch. He had a coolness to him; and he proved by his actions that he guessed all that needed guessing at once. He freed himself from Ives and went rolling off the boardwalk. The buckshot had screamed over their heads; the buckshot spattered against the siding of a building behind them. Carradine quickly got on his hands and knees, then reared himself to a stand. He pulled Ives to his feet and dragged Ives with him, and the two of them went running across the street, running toward the drug-store.

Men were emerging from doorways, drawn by the sound of the gun blast; boots beat along the planking, shrill voices rose. To all cries and questions, Ives was deaf. He gained the doorway of the drugstore, the colonel with him. Now they were directly below the window in Stoll's quarters, and if Stoll had reloaded they might be in their greatest danger. But the door gave to their hands and they were inside and safe from a second blast from overhead.

Ives struggled to speak. Ives gasped, "Have you got a gun?"

The colonel dug an ivory-handled forty-five from beneath his coat; it was the gun he'd slept with many years. The colonel had recovered his aplomb. He said, "I believe our bird has flown, sir. Look, the back door's open."

Ives edged up the stairs to Stoll's quarters. They were deserted; the shotgun lay on the floor, furniture had been overturned by the haste of Stoll's departure, chessmen strewed the floor. Ives came below; he looked out the back door; there was no sign of Stoll.

Ives said, "His nerve gave way when he didn't get you. He's run for it."

Carradine said, "I should have expected Stoll's play. I see that now. How did you know?"

"Men coming," Ives said warningly.

Townsmen crowded the doorway; the colonel looked at them. "An accident," the colonel said. "Nobody's hurt." He waved them away; he shut out their questions with that gesture; he was still the colonel. The men glanced about, their faced ludicrous. They drifted. Ives left the building, the colonel with him. A few paces down the street, Ives put his back to a wall, and the colonel did likewise. Here Ives could look either direction, commanding the street. The colonel carefully brushed the dust from his suit.

"I think, sir," the colonel said, "that you have something to say to me."

Ives said, "He hated you. For what happened on the trail from Texas. And he hated Jim Ives, too, because Jim Ives handled the whip. Not long ago I grabbed Stoll's wrist. It was a thing he couldn't stand. I should have known then that he'd never have forgiven the man who laid a whip on him. And because he hated Jim Ives and you and your son, two of you three died in Dodge."

The colonel's face was heavy with thinking. "How do you make that out?"

"Tom Feather," Ives said. "He went to Dave Carradine's hotel room in Dodge. Jim Ives came there, and Jim Ives was on the prod. When the smoke settled, two men were dead and Tom Feather's memory was gone. But he had his flashes after that. Tell me, was there any way a man could have climbed to the window of that hotel room in Dodge?"

Carradine passed his hand across his forehead. "Possibly. I don't remember."

"Stoll did it, just the same. Stoll came to the window and started shooting. Jim Ives and Dave Carradine didn't shoot at each other; they shot at him. And Tom Feather got caught in the middle of it. Tom, shot to doll ribbons, ever after was addled and therefore not dangerous to Stoll. And Tom had a fear of guns. But the night that he braced Brule in his shack, he was shot again. And that took Tom back to the night in Dodge."

The colonel nodded. "So that is why he pointed to the window and shouted Stoll's name!"

"Exactly," Ives said. "He felt a bullet, and he remembered Marco Stoll at another window long ago."

Carradine said, "My God! My God!"

"Stoll got two of the men he hated in Dodge City. That left you. And it left me, because later he hated me, too. That was because I looked like Jim Ives; you hated me for the same reason. And Stoll had two more of us he wanted dead."

Carradine said, "Stoll's been on this range for many years. Time and again he must have had his chance."

"Yes," Ives said, "but it's my guess that he wanted more than your death. You'd had him stripped down like a peon and lashed to a wheel and flogged. Some men's souls would have healed with their scars; not Stoll's though. Once I told him I'd learned that there were other sicknesses besides those of the flesh. You'd humbled him; he wanted you humbled; he wanted you stripped, too, but in a different fashion. He's a chess player, so he moved pawns. And all of us were the pawns."

"Didn't he befriend you the day you came back to Tamerlane?"

Ives glanced up the street; a few men loitered about; to them, he and the colonel must have seemed two men making idle talk. Ives said, "Yes, he bought in when Cory Lund braced me on the street. But that was Stoll's way of winning my confidence; Stoll had to learn why I'd come back. Because I felt obligated to him, I admitted that Tana had written she needed my help in handling you. Tana wanted you to give up your war against the nesters. That war was something Stoll wished; he was sure you would lose and that way he'd see you brought to your knees. He must have feared that I'd have some influence on you because he tired to talk me into leaving. When I refused, he kept up his pretense by loaning me his buggy. And then he set Brule to lie in wait for me. I was to be killed. I wasn't to be saved for something special as you were."

Carradine said, "Then it must have been Stoll who mailed me the half of the hundred-dollar bill."

"It must have been. It was a shot in the dark, just as you guessed then; there was little lost if it didn't work. Meanwhile, he'd had Brule shoot Cory; that was to be blamed on me, and that was to have set off trouble between nesters and Hammer. Stoll didn't dream that Benedict would be allowed to take me off Hammer; Stoll was mighty surprised when I came riding into town with the sheriff. Later that night he came around and offered to help me break jail. My escape would have been pegged onto Hammer, thereby arousing the nesters. I did escape, but only so I could patch up Cory Lund and stop the war."

Carradine said, "And I raided town!"

"Stoll must have expected that, too, knowing you. But your raid was too late, so he had to make another play. Brule took a second shot at me. Then you held Benedict hostage. When the time came to exchange Tana for Benedict, Stoll was out at the nester settlement. He must have got word to Brule at once. Elisha Lund was shot by Brule, and Tana was carried off, to be held captive for a couple of days. Stoll was really growing desperate when he planned that one. Lund's death was to have aroused the nesters; Tana's disappearance was to have aroused you. But I held off the nesters because they needed me, and you found Tana. Then you gave up the fight. When I heard that, I reasoned that Stoll had likely heard it, too. Once you stepped on that stage, you'd be gone out of Stoll's life. He'd failed in his scheme to break you by forcing you into a lost cause; the only thing left was for him to kill you."

Carradine said slowly, "That was superb reasoning on your part."

"One by one, I picked up the pieces. Tana gave me the last one today when she told me about Tom Feather's dying. When I realized that Stoll had done the killing in Dodge City, I understood everything. And I knew what you were facing."

He looked across the street. "Your stage's about ready to pull out."

Carradine said, "I won't be taking it. We have a hunt to make, you and I."

Ives shook his head. "You really beat Stoll the moment you decided to call off your war. The greatest service you can do Sombra Range is to climb on that stage. I'd like your gun, if you don't mind. You won't need it where you're going."

Carradine's face was uncompromising until a thought softened it. "I dealt you injustice for many years," he said. "Stoll needs only one bullet, and only one man can send it. I owe something to you, and something to Jim Ives." He produced his gun and passed it to Ives; it was the colonel's real surrender; it was the handing over of his way of life. He sighed. "I'm old," he said. "I'm glad to be done with all of it. Perhaps somewhere in the South there'll be a place for me to sit in the sun."

Ives remembered the language of that sun-drenched land. "*Vaya con Dios,*" he said. "Go with God."

Carradine extended his hand. Ives took the hand; it came to him then that he had known this man all his conscious days; he had been closer to the colonel than he had to any other man, yet not until this last parting had they ever shaken hands.

Carradine said, "Good-by, Brian."

They walked across the street together; Ives held open the coach's door. The driver frowned impatiently; he spat tobacco juice; his whip cracked. Ives watched the stage careen away; one of the colonel's thin hands emerged from a window and waved. The sunset caught the coach and made a blur of it; the rattle of wheels died; the dust plume settled.

Ives stood aimlessly; he became aware of the colonel's gun in his hand; he frowned at the weapon; he had been trained to heal, and he held a strange instrument now. He thrust the gun into the waistband of his trousers. Dusk fogged the street; Ives suddenly grew wary of shadows. Hoofs rattled, and he looked up to see Cory Lund leaping down from a lathered horse.

Cory said, "Tana told me you were heading here to stave off some sort of big trouble."

Ives talked; he told Cory a very great deal in a very few words. He finished his talk, and Cory frowned. Cory said, "Stoll's likely still in town. There's a few empty shacks up the street. I'll head that way and look into doors. You go the other way. When you get to your end of the street, turn and head back. I'll meet up with you somewhere."

Ives said, "This isn't your game."

Cory smiled; there was no humor in it. "Have you forgotten Brule? And Elisha Lund?"

Ives said, "If you run into Rod Benedict, tell him what's up."

Cory nodded. "I'll be seeing you."

Ives turned to the first of the saloons; he shouldered the batwings aside and looked at the few men who were liquoring; Stoll was not there. He came back to the planking and glanced toward the Oriental Café, but he judged that Stoll would not be so bold as to be loitering in a public place. Likely Cory's theory concerning the deserted shacks was more nearly correct. Still—

Ives paced along; he turned toward the wooden awning of another saloon, and Charley came lurching out. This was the first time Ives had seen the town drunkard since the day of his return to Tamerlane, but Charley knew him. Charley's breath reeked. Charley said in a hoarse stage whisper, "Stoll's down in Benedict's jail. Now ain't that a place to hide! In a jail!"

Ives fished a dollar from his pocket and passed it to Charley. It jingled against other coins in Charley's pocket, but Ives wasn't to think of that till afterward. He went quick-striding toward the jail; he came into Rod Benedict's office cautiously. Only shadows were here. He moved to the barred cell door and said softly, "Stoll? Marco Stoll?"

Some vast bulk moved in there, and Ives quickly flattened himself against the office wall beside the door. Stoll said wearily, "I'm not armed. I lit out too fast to take the shotgun."

Ives said sharply, "Come out of there!"

Stoll said, "The door's open."

Ives reached and hooked a toe between two of the bars

of the door. He tugged, and the door swung open. He got the colonel's gun in his hand, and he lunged into the cell. Stoll was seated on the bunk; Stoll was a black blotch against blackness. Stoll said, "What are you going to do? Shoot me down?"

Here was surprise; Ives had expected a defiant, fighting Stoll; he had expected to run against the courage of the cornered. He walked across to Stoll; he reached down and patted Stoll's clothes for a weapon. Stoll made no move; Stoll might have been a sack of sawdust. Ives said, "I'm going to light a lamp. I want to be able to watch you."

He stepped out into the sheriff's office and fumbled with the lamp on Benedict's desk. He got it burning and fetched it into the cell and placed it on a stand. Stoll looked at him unblinkingly; Stoll was never more like a toad.

Ives said, "You're in jail now, and you'll stay here until Benedict comes to turn the key."

Stoll lifted his hands and let them drop upon his knees. It was a shrug.

Ives said, "There's one thing I've got to know. What profit was to be in it for you? There wasn't a red cent, so far as I can see. Was it just revenge?"

Stoll's face came to life. It showed hate. He said, "Can't you understand how it piled up as the years went by until it was bigger than a mountain?"

Ives shook his head; he could understand this, yet it was beyond his understanding; it was like sick tissue under a microscope, only it was a man's soul he was seeing. Ives said, "A bullet would have balanced up for you any of the time across the years. But you would have had cattleman pitted against farmer and half a hundred of them dead. All because of something twenty-three years past!"

Stoll said, "And it was all going my way till you came back!"

Ives said, "God, if you knew how sickening you are!"

Stoll lifted his head; Stoll seemed to be listening, and then the awareness of danger was upon Ives like a blanket thrown over him. He remembered Charley's money, and he understood; he knew that Charley had been bribed to tell him that Stoll was here. He realized this just as the gun went off; the gun spoke beyond the cell window; the gun was out there in the weed-choked lot where once Stoll had stood. The gun and a second gun and a hoarse shout and a name said vilely, and the sound of a man falling.

Stoll was upon his feet; Stoll was reaching behind him, and a six-shooter lay on the cot—a six-shooter which Stoll had been sitting upon. Stoll got this gun into his hand, and the lamp flickered with the concussion of his first shot. Ives felt the breath of the bullet; the lead drew splinters from the wall; but Ives was firing then; Ives was making the colonel's gun work, and Stoll folded over and fell into a heap upon the floor.

Boots were stampeding in Benedict's office, and Cory came lunging inside. Cory stood looking at Stoll's body, and Cory said, "I see it now. He was to be the bait to hold you while Brule got in a lick through the window. But their timing went wrong. I got back down the street to find Brule out there skulking around."

Ives looked toward the cell window; he looked out there where Brule had been.

"Dead," Cory said.

Ives let the colonel's gun slip from his fingers, and he put a hand to the wall, feeling very sick. Ives said, "I've had enough for one day."

20
Walls Fallen

THE NESTER HOSPITAL STOOD EMPTY, AND IVES MOVED about the building aimlessly this sunny afternoon. His instrument case was here, and so was his carpetbag; he had come for these things, but with them ready to be removed, he still lingered. He had grown to like this place. He looked at the two rows of empty beds; he had made a good fight here; moreover, he had made friends. In the days since Stoll and Brule had died, Ives had eaten many meals at many different tables. Now the work was done, and now, suddenly, he felt rootless again.

He had his plans made, but there were the little last things to do. He flung his Prince Albert over his arm; he picked up the two bags and went out to the waiting horse. It was a Lund horse; he had long since returned Tana's mount to her. He fastened the bags to the saddle and rode toward Lund's place. The Sombra glinted in the sun; men hailed him in passing as he jogged along; overhead the sky arched blue and cloudless. Here was a land without shadow.

He came to the little cemetery the plague had fashioned;

here stood the monuments to failure, but last night he had delivered a baby for a nester woman, and there was that to remember. The endless circle went on; a doctor could only lessen the pain. Sometimes he felt a cheat when men lifted their hands in respectful salute to him.

He might have said good-by as he moved from place to place; he didn't do this. The good-bys would be only for those who had touched him closely. That made part of his reason why he was going to Lund's.

He reached the place in late afternoon; silence droned in the yard; a hundred memories lingered here. He came down from the horse in the shadow of one of the outbuildings; he walked toward the shack and heard voices. Rod Benedict was here. Benedict, Ives judged, was sitting on a bench before the place. Benedict was saying, "This range has got so quiet I'm thinking of asking the taxpayers to hire me a deputy. I need somebody to play checkers with."

Marybelle's laughter came. Marybelle must be standing in the doorway of the shack. She said, "I'm no good at the game, but I could try."

Benedict held silent a moment. Then he said, "Would it be seemly if I came out here often? It's been mighty lonesome since Maw took off for Kansas. Sometimes a man just needs somebody to talk to."

Marybelle said, "You come as often as you like."

Ives felt like an eavesdropper, yet because his thoughts always turned inward, he reflected that here was rightness he hadn't perceived. He had never thought of Benedict and Marybelle together, but now he saw the sense of it. Benedict was a man of courage and energy, but there was a certain aimlessness to him. He needed his footsteps directed, and he had found a girl who would direct them. Yet there was one thing Ives didn't understand, surely Benedict knew that the colonel was no longer at Hammer.

Ives coughed and made unnecessary commotion with his feet and came around the corner of the shack. Marybelle straightened herself in the doorway; Benedict looked up lazily. Ives said, "I just stopped by to say I'll be taking the horse into Tamerlane, if you don't mind. I'll leave him at the livery stable."

Marybelle's eyes clouded. "You're going, then?"

Ives nodded. "Back to Oregon. On tonight's stage." He made his voice very casual. "I just stopped by to say so long. Cory around?"

"He's out riding."

Ives said, "Tell him good-by for me," and his thought was that there was no need for words between him and Cory; their kinship had been forged by the plague and gotten its last tempering in Tamerlane's jail building when two men had died.

Marybelle traced a pattern on the doorstep with her toe. "Does Tana know?"

"I haven't seen her lately," Ives said and wondered if the pain showed in his eyes.

Benedict pulled himself to a stand. "I'll be riding along," he said. He came close to Ives; he looked at Ives broodingly for a moment, then made a fist of his right hand and beat it softly against Ives's shoulder. He grinned at Ives, and the grin made him boyish again.

Benedict said, "Oh, hell, Doc, how could I hate you if I tried?"

Ives said, "That's one of the good things that have come out of all this."

Benedict walked to his horse and climbed into the saddle. Marybelle called after him. "You come back. Rod. Soon."

Benedict lifted his hand and trotted the horse out of the yard. Marybelle watched him speculatively, and Ives waited out the moment and said, "You won't bag him easily. Tana's free now. Are you very sure he's what you want?''

She said, ''He'll tie me here, to this land. But you guessed once that I'd never get away, not really. Maybe you knew me better than I knew myself.'' She smiled at Ives; she summoned the old roguishness. ''So it's good-by, Doc.''

Part of her would ride with him always; he knew that now. They had been too close too many times. He opened his arms; she came into them. He kissed her gently, not holding her long. He said, ''Be good to him, Marybelle. If you get him, you'll have yourself a boy to raise.''

She said, ''You be good to yourself, Doc.'' She blinked. ''Damn you, Doc,'' she said.

He walked to the horse, not looking back. He took himself across the yard, and when he was in the saddle and up the lift, he lingered a moment, gazing at Elisha Lund's grave. It would look fine with a monument some day, he reflected, but there was already a monument, and he had built his part of it. That was good.

He rode along slowly; he had all the time in the world now, and his pace suited his mood. Always there was the Sombra shining in the sunlight; the banked willows danced faintly in reflection; there was no more shadow than that. And that, too, was good. He came to the cutbank where Brule had waylaid him; he felt sorry for Brule, who had spun out his days in futility and died by the means of his living. He remembered the rattlesnake. The biter had indeed got bitten.

Tamerlane was hazed by dusk when he reached the town; he came first to the stage station and bought a ticket to railhead; he found that he had nearly an hour of waiting. He led the Lund horse down the street to the livery and arranged for the mount to be kept till Cory could come after it. This was the first time he'd been in the livery since the day of his return to Tamerlane. The timelessness of the place impressed him again; the horses still stood listlessly in their stalls; the air was heavy with the smell of them. He walked out into the street. A wagon rolled along, a man and woman and child upon the seat, spooled barbed wire filling the wagon box.

Once before he'd stepped from the livery stable and there'd been a nester wagon with this same cargo; and now this gave him a start—this was too much like the other day. But the man at the reins was Beamis; Beamis noticed him and sawed at the reins and said, "Good evening, Doc."

Ives walked over to the wagon. The little girl was emaciated from the fever; the little girl was all eyes.

Beamis said, "They tell it that you're leaving us, Doc."

Ives nodded. "Tonight's stage."

Beamis looked out across the land; Beamis looked to where the Sombra Hills lifted. "You come back any time, Doc. We'll always find room for you."

"I'll remember that," Ives said.

He moved along the planking; Stoll's drugstore was dark; a new man was coming to take over. Also, a new doctor was coming to Sombra Range. Thus had Ives's last usefulness here dissolved.

He saw Charley seated aimlessly on the edge of the boardwalk, his feet a tangle before him. He remembered that Charley had been paid to toll him into the death trap Marco Stoll had prepared. He spoke to Charley in passing; he forgave Charley. He turned in at the Oriental Café and had a meal, lingering over it. He had been so busy for so long that this wealth of time seemed a burden to him; all things were aimless.

The luggage was loaded when he came back to the stagecoach; the driver was climbing aloft. Ives stored his carpetbag in the rack overhead, but he kept his instrument case in his hand. The case he took with him inside the coach; there was only one other passenger; she was seated in the far corner; she wore a trailing dress that rustled with her slightest movement; a plumed hat shadowed her face.

Ives said, "Tana!"

The driver's whip cracked; the coach lurched forward, wheeling along the street. Ives raised his voice above this clamor. He said, "You're going, too?"

"Wherever you're going, Brian."

He carefully put the instrument case down on the floor between his feet. He let his hands lie aimlessly in his lap. He could find no words.

She said, "Why didn't you come to me, Brian? Cory told me about Stoll—and the finish. Up till that day, this was impossible for both of us, I know. There were Jim Ives and Dave Carradine, and we'd have had them to shadow us all our days. But when the truth came out about Marco Stoll, the last wall came tumbling down."

He said, "Yes, I know. But what about Benedict?"

She said, "It was lonely on Hammer. When Benedict rode for us, there was someone on the place to remind me that I was a woman. Yes, we made the motions of being in love. That was good for me. But you were there, somewhere in a corner of my heart, always—that lonely boy I'd cried for. Marybelle Lund knew how I felt—she must have read it in my face the night I came to Feather's place to tell you about the trouble. That's why she couldn't be friendly with me."

He said helplessly. "But it was always Benedict you were concerned about. Take that day he put himself into danger by coming to Hammer to arrest me—"

She said softly, "Don't we owe something to those who love us, Brian?"

He looked out the window; they were beyond Tamerlane; the road snaked across an expanse of prairie and the yesterdays were dropping behind them. He looked and understood everything then; he had had a kinship with this girl, always, and even their years apart hadn't changed that. She had lived for the colonel, and lately she had lived for Rod Benedict, while he, Ives, had lived for myriad patients who'd taken their toll on him. That had been their lot, sacrificing themselves for the good of others. They were of a kind, and they had found each other now, and the wonder of that, the miracle, was too big for easy grasping.

Tana said, "Rod came to me after the colonel left for Texas. I told him how it was with me. He came again today, to tell me that you were leaving. When you didn't come to say good-by, I knew you hadn't really understood. That left me only this to do."

He said, "I haven't much for you in Oregon."

She said, "You have you."

He remembered Marybelle saying, "You'd give me the real security that all of us are after—the security of knowing I was owned and would therefore be protected because I'd be the most priceless of all properties. Yes, Doc, I'll have security when I have you—" He had learned from Marybelle; he was grateful to her.

He said, "We can be married before we catch the train."

They both fell silent; if she shared the yearning that was suddenly in him, she didn't show it; and he supposed that it was the same with her as it was with him; he wanted to taste the wonder of this, he wanted to taste anticipation.

He said presently, "I've been thinking. If it hadn't been for Stoll, I might have been raised like a true son of the colonel. Then I'd have likely stayed at Hammer and turned cattleman; and when the nesters came, I'd have reasoned as the colonel reasoned. And so it might have all been different—for myself and for this range. Perhaps I owed Stoll something. At least I owe him forgiveness."

She said, "You'll always find the good in all things. I'll try to be good for you, Brian. Will you kiss me now?"

He took her in his arms; her hat was in his way; he loosened the ribbon and tipped the hat back; it fell unheeded. First he kissed her eyes, and then her lips. She sighed; her sigh was long and trembling. She rested in his arms, and he held her thus, and time lost its meaning, and he felt like weeping; he felt that he should be down upon his knees.